MACMILLAN MODERN NOVELISTS

General Editor: Norman Page

MACMILLAN MODERN NOVELISTS

MACMILLAN MODERN NOVELISTS

H. G. WELLS

Michael Draper

MACMILLAN

First published 1987

Published by
Higher and Further Education Division
MACMILLAN PUBLISHERS LTD
Houndmills, Basingstoke, Hampshire RG21 2XS
and London
Companies and representatives
throughout the world

Typeset by
Wessex Typesetters
(Division of The Eastern Press Ltd)
Frome, Somerset

Printed in Hong Kong

British Library Cataloguing in Publication Data
Draper, Michael
H. G. Wells.
1. Wells, H. G.—Criticism and
interpretation
I. Title
823'912   PR5777
ISBN 0–333–40746–6
ISBN 0–333–40747–4 Pbk

11397616

Series Standing Order

If you would like to receive future titles in this series as they are
published, you can make use of our standing order facility. To place a
standing order please contact your bookseller or, in case of difficulty,
write to us at the address below with your name and address and the
name of the series. Please state with which title you wish to begin your
standing order. (If you live outside the United Kingdom we may not
have the rights for your area, in which case we will forward your order
to the publisher concerned.)

Customer Services Department, Macmillan Distribution Ltd
Houndmills, Basingstoke, Hampshire, RG21 2XS, England.

Contents

Acknowledgments

Acknowledgment is gratefully made to the Estate of H. G. Wells for permission to quote from Wells's works.

My thanks go also to the following people, without whose aid and encouragement the present study would not have reached its present form: John Lucas and Tom Paulin for successively supervising my doctoral thesis at Nottingham University, from which much of the material in the book is drawn; Colin Harrison of the University's Education Department for practical assistance with submission of the thesis; the staff of Bromley Central Library for courteous, efficient access to their Wells Collection; and also the many members of the H. G. Wells Society from whose zeal and insight I have benefited, among them Christopher Rolfe, David Smith, David Jarrett, Sonia Burgess, John Hammond and, above all, Patrick Parrinder, who read through the typescript and offered many valuable suggestions. Additional thanks go to John Harper for help with the proof-reading. It may be, however, that the greatest debt is the one I owe Iain Zaczek, who over the years has fortified me time and again with staunch friendship and innumerable cups of coffee.

General Editor's Preface

The death of the novel has often been announced, and part of the secret of its obstinate vitality must be its capacity for growth, adaptation, self-renewal and even self-transformation: like some vigorous organism in a speeded-up Darwinian ecosystem, it adapts itself quickly to a changing world. War and revolution, economic crisis and social change, radically new ideologies such as Marxism and Freudianism, have made this century unprecedented in human history in the speed and extent of change, but the novel has shown an extraordinary capacity to find new forms and techniques and to accommodate new ideas and conceptions of human nature and human experience, and even to take up new positions on the nature of fiction itself.

In the generations immediately preceding and following 1914, the novel underwent a radical redefinition of its nature and possibilities. The present series of monographs is devoted to the novelists who created the modern novel and to those who, in their turn, either continued and extended, or reacted against and rejected, the traditions established during that period of intense exploration and experiment. It includes a number of those who lived and wrote in the nineteenth century but whose innovative contribution to the art of fiction makes it impossible to ignore them in any account of the origins of the modern novel; it also includes the so-called 'modernists' and those who in the mid- and late twentieth century have emerged as outstanding practitioners of this genre. The scope is, inevitably, international; not only, in the migratory and exile-haunted world of our century, do writers refuse to heed national frontiers – 'English' literature lays claim to Conrad the Pole, Henry James the American, and Joyce the Irishman – but geniuses such as Flaubert, Dostoevski and Kafka have had an influence on the fiction of many nations.

Each volume in the series is intended to provide an introduction to the fiction of the writer concerned, both for those approaching him or her for the first time and for those who are already familiar with some parts of the achievement in question and now wish to place it in the context of the total *oeuvre*. Although essential information relating to the writer's life and times is given, usually in an opening chapter, the approach is primarily critical and the emphasis is not upon 'background' or generalisations but upon close examination of important texts. Where an author is notably prolific, major texts have been selected for detailed attention but an attempt has also been made to convey, more summarily, a sense of the nature and quality of the author's work as a whole. Those who want to read further will find suggestions in the select bibliography included in each volume. Many novelists are, of course, not only novelists but also poets, essayists, biographers, dramatists, travel writers and so forth; many have practised shorter forms of fiction; and many have written letters or kept diaries that constitute a significant part of their literary output. A brief study cannot hope to deal with all these in detail, but where the shorter fiction and the non-fictional writings, public and private, have an important relationship to the novels, some space has been devoted to them.

NORMAN PAGE

Abbreviations

Atlantic Edition
   The Works of H. G. Wells: Atlantic Edition, 28 volumes (London:
   Unwin, 1924–7)
Bergonzi
   Bernard Bergonzi, *The Early H. G. Wells* (Manchester:
   Manchester University Press, 1961)
Blake
   William Blake, *Complete Writings*, Geoffrey Keynes (ed.)
   (London: Oxford University Press, 1974 edition)
Critical Essays
   Bernard Bergonzi (ed.), *H. G. Wells: A Collection of Critical
   Essays* (Englewood Cliffs, N.J.: Prentice-Hall, 1976)
Critical Heritage
   Patrick Parrinder (ed.), *H. G. Wells: The Critical Heritage*
   (London: Routledge & Kegan Paul, 1972)
EA
   H. G. Wells, *Experiment in Autobiography* (London: Gollancz &
   Gresset, 1934)
Early Writings
   H. G. Wells: Early Writings in Science and Science Fiction, Robert
   M. Philmus and David Y. Hughes (eds.) (Berkeley and
   London: University of California, 1975)
Literary Criticism
   H. G. Wells's Literary Criticism, Patrick Parrinder and Robert
   M. Philmus (eds.) (Brighton: Harvester, 1980)
MacKenzie
   Norman and Jeanne MacKenzie, *The Time Traveller* (London:
   Weidenfeld & Nicolson, 1973)
Parrinder
   Patrick Parrinder, *H. G. Wells* (Edinburgh: Oliver & Boyd,
   1970)

For my mother

1
Beginnings: Wells's Life

H. G. Wells is a writer with several, almost rival, identities: science fiction author, comic novelist, social novelist, controversialist, forecaster of the future and historian of mankind. The quantity of his work is no less remarkable than its breadth. Wells averaged two books annually, plus pamphlets and other journalism, for fifty-three years.

Despite the customary critical reservations – that the connections between life and art are not strictly provable, and that fiction must be appreciated on its own merits, not for what it tells us about its author – Wells's life remains stubbornly pertinent to his art, both as its original context and as the source of much of its subject-matter.

Herbert George Wells was born on 21 September 1866 in Bromley, Kent, the youngest of three brothers. His mother, Sarah, was a former lady's maid; his father, Joseph, was a former gardener. Mr Wells senior ran a shop selling crockery, china, glassware and cricket goods, and worked as a professional cricketer whenever he was able, but neither business brought in much money. Although his wife struggled to maintain the family's middle class status, sending her sons to a tiny private school for tradesmen, the Wellses were poor. They became more so in 1877 when a broken leg deprived Mr Wells of his cricketing income.

In 1880 Mrs Wells was able to partly remedy matters by finding a post as housekeeper at Uppark, a country house in Sussex, and sending thirteen-year-old Bertie out to work. The boy was far from happy with this arrangement. Having been extremely successful at school, he was keen to get a formal education. He found himself instead shunted into a series of menial jobs, in a drapery, a school run by a distant relative with forged qualifications, a chemist's shop, then another drapery.

Only compensatory daydreams and occasional visits to Uppark relieved the drudgery of these unpromising beginnings. Freedom to roam a country house and its grounds made a striking contrast to confinement in an apprentices' dormitory. That such a fulfilling environment could be created provoked his wonder; that it was reserved for others, his enmity.

The irreverent view of his superiors and great love of reading which he had developed made him seize eagerly on the Uppark library, where he enjoyed particularly the imaginative satire and social criticism of Swift, Voltaire and Thomas Paine. Back at work, he devoted much of his leisure time to studying popular encyclopedias, desperate to keep in touch with the world of learning. Like many other late-Victorians, he was fascinated by the way the findings and methods of science cast doubt on old religious assumptions and suggested possibilities of changing the human condition. For most of the thinking public the prospect was painful, but Wells was keen to embrace all things revolutionary. He had already rebelled against his mother's piety, perceiving her religious faith to be the official mythology of the social order which had labelled him fit for menial tasks only.

In 1882 came a chance to escape that depressing future. Horace Byatt, headmaster of Midhurst Grammar School, had taught Wells some Latin during his abortive chemist's apprenticeship. Impressed by his brainpower and enthusiasm, Byatt agreed to offer him a student assistantship, taking him on at the school as both teacher and pupil. Although Wells's parents were financially committed to their son's continuation at the Southsea Drapery Emporium, Wells himself was sure he had found a new beginning which would lead him somewhere worthwhile. To him this was a life-or-death struggle. He fought their resistance with rational arguments and with a threat of suicide.

When his parents eventually gave in, he was rewarded for his determination by greater success than even he had foreseen. His efficiency in passing examinations led within a year to an offer of a state scholarship to the Normal School of Science in South Kensington (now Imperial College, part of London

University), where he would be able to attend lectures by T. H. Huxley, Darwin's champion. Wells had fought his way out of the drapery just in time to become one of the first scholarship boys. The experience reinforced his belief in state intervention and science as twin agents of change for the better.

Yet, after a productive first year as a student, Wells once more displayed the deep restlessness which would be characteristic of him all his life. He neglected his scientific studies to read Romantic literature, especially Blake and Carlyle, two fervent opponents of scientific materialism. He became more visibly a socialist, equipping himself with a red tie and attending public meetings. He helped found a magazine and a debating society at the college, clowned around in class and, perhaps the most fundamental distraction of all, fell in love with his cousin Isabel Wells.

The result was that he left college in 1887 without a degree and was reduced to teaching in small private schools. Playing a game of soccer at a particularly grim one in Wales, he received a foul from a boy which damaged one of his kidneys. A series of lung haemorrhages combined with this injury to make him a periodic invalid for over ten years. During his initial recovery Wells began to work more seriously at his writing. He attempted both verse and fiction and studied several authors, Hawthorne and Stevenson among them. However, the prospect of belatedly getting his degree, which he finally did in 1890, offered him a more practical route to an income than authorship.

He became a biology tutor for a correspondence-course-cum-private-college, teaching, editing the house journal and contributing to several educational papers. He was able to marry Isabel in 1891. When in 1893 two books appeared with the name "H. G. Wells" on the title page, one of them a collaboration, they were not novels but biology textbooks. It seemed the misfit had at last found a congenial place in life. Yet, just beneath the surface, dissatisfaction persisted. In particular he was soon disillusioned with his marriage. Finding his wife tamely conventional in her attitudes and sexually unresponsive to him, he quickly turned to other women for consolation.

In the same year that his textbooks were published, a further haemorrhage brought him close to death. The fear that he had little time to live resolved him to break out into a better life while he still could. He ran off with one of his students, Amy Catherine Robbins, and embarked on a career as a professional writer. Although he had sold some essays written during his recent convalescence, he had no way of knowing whether he could build on that success. Fortunately there was a boom in the market for light journalism and fiction. For it Wells eagerly poured out essays, book reviews, theatre reviews, speculative articles on science and short stories.

At the suggestion of the great editor W. E. Henley, Wells used a series of his science articles as the basis for the novella many consider to be his most original and best crafted work, *The Time Machine*. By 1895, when he was divorced from Isabel and married to Catherine, or "Jane" as he preferred to call her, he had followed up this success by producing a satirical fantasy, *The Wonderful Visit*, and a second venture into science fiction, *The Island of Doctor Moreau*. These were soon followed by a comic novel, *The Wheels of Chance*, and two further scientific romances, *The Invisible Man* and *The War of the Worlds*.

The early scientific romances made Wells's name and remain his most celebrated achievement but, surprising as it may seem, their author was keen to move away from them toward another kind of fiction, one which would let him live up to his responsibilities as a public figure as he understood these and perhaps gain him greater respect. The works of this second phase try to bring the issues they raise to an explicit and positive conclusion, even at the risk of a conflict between "message" and art. Since Wells's imagination was essentially subversive and concerned with the particular, while his political ideals were general and somewhat authoritarian in approach, such a conflict was hard to avoid. The problem is amply evident in *When the Sleeper Wakes*, the first of the new-style scientific romances. Wells was not unaware of it, but could draw confidence from a flourishing career which was about to bring him a huge international readership through translation.

In 1898 continuing poor health led him to move to Sandgate on the Kentish coast, where he was able to add to the literary friendships he had already made with Arnold Bennett and George Gissing those of Henry James and Joseph Conrad, both of whom he had vigorously defended as a reviewer and both of whom were now virtually his neighbours. He finished a realistic novel drawing on his experiences as a student, *Love and Mr*

Lewisham, while maintaining his science fiction output with *The First Men in the Moon*.

A visible seal was put on his success when he moved into a fine modern dwelling, Spade House, built to his own specifications. It was designed to suit a resident in a wheelchair since he expected his condition to deteriorate, but in fact his health bloomed with his fame and fortune. He became the father of two sons, George Philip and Frank, in 1901 and 1903 respectively. Their arrival revived what he called his 'domestic claustrophobia, the fear of being caught in a household' (*EA* Ch. 7:4). Hs reaction to the birth of 'Gip', for example, was to vanish on a two-month holiday. The marriage held together largely because of Jane's willingness to tolerate his freedom of movement and his numerous affairs with other women in return for a share of his success.

This was a better bargain than it may sound. Writing before the electronic media substantially diminished public interest in the printed word, Wells could appeal to a greater, more heavily dependent audience than any modern counterpart. He soon realised that, like him, a lot of this audience was curious about the century now beginning, with its prospects of ever-faster social and technological development. Wells's social mobility, scientific training and gift for explanation allowed him to plausibly present himself to them as the prototypical twentieth-century man. His first attempt to annex the future, *Anticipations*, was so well received, he was emboldened to produce further articles, pamphlets and books on the subject. All were built around one central idea: that the growth of communication and transport facilities, which by 'shrinking' the world was responsible for modern social tensions and conflicts, might in the longer term, under the direction of a technocratic elite, make possible a just, efficient world order.

Until the Great War, Wells regarded such writings as an occasional supplement to his main work, which was definitely that of an 'imaginative writer' (*A Modern Utopia*, 'Note to the Reader'). His active involvement in politics was largely confined within the socialist Fabian Society, which he joined in 1903. The playwright George Bernard Shaw, one of its leading members and Wells's lifelong intellectual sparring partner, fought against his repeated attempts to expand the Fabians from a progressive 'think tank' into a full scale revolutionary intelligentsia. After a two-month respite in 1906 while Wells was visiting the USA, interviewing President Theodore Roosevelt *en route*, Shaw finally won the battle, leaving Wells to gradually withdraw from Fabian commitments.

Wells's involvement with radical politics did little to slow down his production of fiction, but helped confirm its change of direction. The notion of an ideal society – how it might be brought about, what it might be like – became central to his work. The openly discursive *Modern Utopia* proved a more suitable vehicle for the question than the scientific romances *The Food of the Gods* and *In the Days of the Comet*. Only *The War in the Air*, a vision of the coming world wars, stands comparison with the earlier science fiction. Deservedly Wells's best-known books of the Edwardian period are his comic novels *Kipps* and *The History of Mr Polly*, portraits of eccentric rebels strugging to escape from a repressive society. Wells's own experiences and feelings memorably animate these books, as they do his foremost social novel, *Tono-Bungay*.

In early 1909 Wells ran off to France with Amber Reeves, a young Fabian who was carrying his child. This time, however, he failed to follow his escape through. Before their daughter Anna-Jane was born, they had returned and Amber had wedded a less encumbered admirer. The controversy which raged around Wells was due not so much to his adultery, which was kept from the general public, as to his latest novel, *Ann Veronica*, in which a heroine resembling Amber flirts with feminism and courts a married man. The furore increased the sales of Wells's books but made it hard for him to find a British publisher for *The New Machiavelli*, a novel about a politician torn between public commitments and his mistress. Not altogether surprisingly, the book is flawed by lack of perspective and long, incoherent arguments. In this, unfortunately, it is representative of most of Wells's later fiction and so marks the close of his second literary phase.

Of the subsequent novels, *Mr Britling Sees It Through*, with its vivid account of life on the home front during the Great War, is the most notable. *Bealby, Joan and Peter, Men Like Gods, The Dream, Christina Alberta's Father* and *Mr Blettsworthy on Rampole Island* may also interest whose who have read Wells's earlier books and wish to try more. While some of the 1920s fiction does have real merit, much of it reworks old ideas with dwindling artistic power. The novels of the 1930s may in my judgement be ignored by all except the specialist. Only when Wells returned directly to his formative experiences in the *Experiment in Autobiography* did he really recover inspiration.

This is not to suggest that the remainder of Wells's life was uneventful. Quite the contrary. If called upon to impress someone with Wells's achievements up to 1915, you would list what he wrote; after that date, you would turn to his activities as a public figure. Since these activities come after his best writings they fall outside the scope of the present book and a brief summary must suffice here.

Through his fifties, sixties and seventies Wells remained remarkably industrious, as an author, an agitator and a lover. (The writer Rebecca West bore him his fourth and last child, Anthony, on the day the Great War began.) Wells supported the 1914–18 war in the hope that ultimately good could be salvaged from it. Correctly believing the nations involved would become more collectivised and efficient, and hoping this would enable the Allies to establish a just and secure world order, he campaigned for a League of Nations and was for a time in charge of the Committee for Propaganda in Enemy Country. The mounting slaughter drove him to seek redemption for individual suffering through religious belief. His theological manifesto *God the Invisible King* dismayed the orthodox and later embarrassed Wells himself, whose godliness proved strictly temporary. His faith in the war waned also, as he realised that the aims of the war leaders and his cosmopolitan ideals did not after all coincide.

In the end the war confirmed Wells's belief that history had become 'a race between education and catastrophe' (*Outline of History* Ch. 41:4). If there were more such international conflicts, with increasingly destructive weapons, civilisation itself would be threatened. Wells produced his *Outline of History* to help disseminate a more global outlook. He feared it would make a loss but it became a bestseller, with two million volumes sold in Britain and the USA alone. In due course outlines of biology and economics followed: *The Science of Life*, written in collaboration with T. H. Huxley's grandson, Julian Huxley, and Wells's son, G. P. Wells, and *The Work, Wealth and Happiness of Mankind*, written with the assistance of Amber Reeves. Characteristically Wells supplemented those tomes with an outrageously bold 'history' of the next couple of centuries, *The Shape of Things to Come*.

The latter was adapted for the screen in 1936 as *Things to Come*, the most memorable of Wells's incursions into the cinema. Its air-raid sequence in particular haunted Britain in the run-up to World War Two. Wells's script coarsens his utopianism to the point of self-parody in a misguided attempt to reach a mass audience, but there are moments when the music and images are quite impressively integrated, especially in a rebuilding-of-civilisation sequence which owed much to Wells's artistic intervention.

The progressive causes and organisations Wells supported in the years between the wars were legion, ranging from free speech to birth control, from the Labour Party to the British Diabetic Association. On behalf of them he sat on committees, made donations, signed petitions, wrote prefaces, broadcast on radio and lectured all around the world. He visited Russia before and after the 1917 revolution; on the second occasion he argued with Lenin and addressed the Petrograd soviet. In 1934 he interviewed F. D. Roosevelt and Joseph Stalin, trying to persuade the US and Soviet leaders that they led societies of a potentially similar nature where the true agents of progress were the technical intelligentsia.

With the coming of the Second World War, Wells embarked on his last major campaign, for the clear formulation of post-war human rights. He was a key figure behind the Sankey Declaration of Rights, a forerunner of the United Nations declaration.

Since Wells believed the desire to be remembered by posterity was unhealthy and in the perspective of cosmic time absurd, it is fitting that he left no gravestone. Instead, after his death on 13 August 1946, his body was cremated and the ashes were scattered over the sea off the South Coast.

Several patterns from this long and eventful life carry into the books which are its testament. Perhaps the most obvious is a recurrent desire for clean starts, and a reluctant recognition that each of these rebirths must become another kind of dead-end. The only way out of the cycle – for Wells, his characters or society at large – seems to be to hitch inner restlessness to a transcendent project. Thus in the *Experiment in Autobiography* Wells traces his career from his first beginnings as a squalling baby in the basement of the family shop, upward and outward through his quest for personal fulfilment, to an eventual recognition of, identification with and contribution to the course of human history. Unfortunately, while his final ascent into these well-meaning generalities may have done something to satisfy Wells the man, it correspondingly diminished the power of Wells the writer, whose work was most alive when he was struggling with his own contradictions, such as his desire for contradictory extremes of freedom and order.

The need to get his feelings and formative experiences into contexts which would give them meaning beyond themselves made Wells impatient with the limits of art. At the same time the need to do justice to those experiences from within repeatedly lured him back into fiction. Achieving some imaginative interaction between the two desires and their contrasting perspectives was essential to the success of his writing. This constant circling round the inner world of art and the outer world of science and politics, never quite willing to embrace the constraints of either, makes Wells a difficult writer to label.

Resistance to categorisation is clearly another characteristic the works share with the life. Wells was no more a conventional novelist than he was a conventional married man. His books have the realistic surface detail and middle-class ambience we associate with the novel, but these features are deliberately disrupted by outlandish fantasy or argument, which brazenly question received notions of relevance and decorum.

Deciding where the innovation ends and incoherence sets in is a major task for any reader of Wells. In understanding and evaluating his work we must be prepared to accept that there are real and important connections between the meanings we produce when we select and shape information into news, politics, history or myth and the meanings we create when we make up stories for entertainment; but equally we must retain a firm grasp on how their various truths to life differ.

Merely swotting up on Wells's opinions cannot prepare us for the task of reading him with due discrimination. The labels again fail to stick, so that unguarded statements about his ideas have a disconcerting tendency to hold true when reversed. He was a utopian; he was a cosmic pessimist. He was an individualist and an authoritarian, an atheist and a religious prophet. To understand the dynamic of Wells's ideas and the curious paradoxes which underlie his fiction, we must examine in more detail how his view of the world developed.

2

A Philosophical Desperado: Wells's Outlook

Three competing sets of attitudes or ways of thinking can be traced in Wells's work. One is a utopian idealism, given plausibility by science but basically derived from Christianity and Plato, which looks forward to the destruction of the present world and its replacement by a better. The second is a down-to-earth scepticism, incorporating science's view of mankind as a natural phenomenon much like any other. The third is a storyteller's delight in recording and transforming every-day reality through the power of his words. All three sets of attitudes are present in Wells's work at all times. In different phases of his career he combined them in different ways, how-ever, and as he varied the mix, he produced radically different results.

The utopian element, which came to be more and more prominent in his work as the years passed, owed much of its shape to his adolescent reading of Plato's *Republic*. Like many of the books which influenced him, he first came upon this discussion of an ideal society in the library of Uppark. For an intelligent and assertive youngster who had been born at the lowest end of the middle class, and who under his parents' guidance was now lurching from one unsatisfactory position in life to another, its classic vision of an orderly meritocracy was inspiring. In the Republic exceptionally gifted children from below can be secretly admitted to the ruling class. Otherwise class boundaries are kept rigid by strict work-specialisation, while the family and every other relation between the sexes is organised in a rational manner. In Wells's fertile mind such revolutionary ideas came together with Uppark itself, as it might have been in its aristocratic heyday, to form an image of an ideal future, a future which might in due course be created through the growth of science and socialism.

In linking his private rebellion to the growing socialist movement, which he first approached through the writings of the American land-socialist pioneer Henry George, Wells was seeking a way out of his individual isolation and powerlessness. Did not the socialists, as much as Plato and himself, aim to abolish private property and promote the common good? When it came to the wish they professed for more democratic ideas and institutions, Wells found the socialists less attractive. He could sympathise easily enough with rebels against upper-class privilege, but he was always equally repelled by the thought of disorderly masses dragging the exceptional down to their level. Wells preferred the idea of a revolution planned and carried out by a group like the Guardians, the elite corps of Plato's Republic.

Labour-movement socialism was foreign to Wells's outlook because it grew out of social conditions foreign to his experience. Plato's utopianism was easy to assimilate since it could be matched to Christian ideas of the end of the world which he had taken in at his mother's knee. The spectacular breakdown of normal existence, the emergence of a formerly oppressed group as an elite and the implementation of absolute justice are particular features of Judaeo-Christian mythology easily transposed into utopian terms.

In his autobiography Wells lays emphasis on his youthful rebellion against Christianity but admits he is still unsure whether to call himself 'an outright atheist or an extreme heretic' (*EA* Ch. 8:3). As a child he accepted the literal truth of Christian myth and fiercely resented it. Because he was a wilful boy whom God was summoned up to quell, religion loomed over him as an all-powerful system hostile to his struggle for fulfilment. Man seemed totally at the mercy of a despotic maker with any hope of redemption far outweighed by the terrible prospect of damnation. A nightmare of 'Our Father in a particularly malignant phase, busy basting a poor broken sinner' haunted him day and night until suddenly, as he says, 'the light broke through to me and I knew this God was a lie' (*EA* Ch. 2:4).

When 'the light broke through' to him (a religious expression deftly perverted) Wells was too young to reject Christianity intellectually. He rejected it imaginatively, willing it to be untrue and belittling it with irreverence. Even half a century after the event he continues to mock, using the ironic title 'Our Father' to deface an image which still has some power over him. In truth Wells's childhood anti-epiphany left him not so much an atheist as an ex-Christian. Between the ages of fourteen and sixteen, he tells us, he meditated, read the anti-Christian weekly the *Freethinker* and attended services of various denominations. He was still looking, in other words, for some form of salvation.

Seen from this angle, Plato's utopia appealed to him not only as a suggestive political ideal but as an acceptable equivalent to heaven. The idea of a perfect future could offer consolation and confer a much-needed significance on his rootless life without demanding that he surrender to an all-powerful, all-knowing god or defer his hope of fulfilment to a supernatural world. Having previously rejected Christianity as a mythology of oppression, Wells found he could substitute utopianism as a mythology of liberation. The ideal state, devised by man and sought in this world, became his ultimate goal.

This does not mean Wells took over Plato's ideas uncritically. Far from it. Plato's utopianism may dispense with gods, but it still depends on belief in an unseen world, a belief which Wells decisively rejected.

Plato reasons on the basis of necessary truths or universals: general terms like 'justice', 'roundness' and 'chair'. He does not see these as mental constructs, bringing out the implicit relations between particular facts, but as the names of actual things. Since absolute justice, a perfect circle and an ideal chair are not to be found in human experience, it follows, according to Plato, that these latent realities constitute a transcendent order, of which earthly existence is an inferior replica.

Belief that utopia must be in harmony with that one perfect order leads logically to totalitarianism. Fiction and drama have to be prohibited in case they distract the citizens from the ideal and offer them inferior models of behaviour. Even some kinds of music are avoided since they rouse emotions and attitudes at odds with the maintenance of stability. There is no question of individuals being allowed to pursue original ideas or private desires; these would always lead them away from the theoretical perfection. Plato's ideal state is by definition what Sir Karl Popper has termed a 'closed society'.[1]

The famous parable with which Book Seven of Plato's *Republic* begins affirms an unswerving loyalty to the absolute. Plato compares ordinary people to prisoners bound in a cave, able to see only the shadows cast on a wall by a fire behind them whenever anything is passed in front of it. The philosopher is one free to get up and look for the hidden reality. Unfortunately when the philosopher comes back into the depths of the cave, the world of experience and common sense, the dim light causes him to blunder and he is mocked by the vulgar rather than hailed as a man of genuine vision.

Wells's short story 'The Country of the Blind' is a reworking of this parable, as Bertrand Russell first pointed out.[2] In Wells's tale Nunez, a mountaineer, falls into an isolated South American valley occupied by blind people. Recalling the proverb 'In the country of the blind, the one-eyed man is King', he assumes he will be able to impose his superior understanding on them, and with it his rule. Instead he is regarded as sub-human and forced to respect the conventions of the blind. At the prospect of having his eyes put out to ensure conformity, he finally flees back into the mountains, apparently to a welcome death.

Plato's allegory forces a conflict of outlooks into totally opposite terms: light and darkness, right and wrong. Wells's story presents a more subtle picture. His comparatively realistic presentation, with its emphasis on the value of sight, directs our imaginative interest to persons, objects and events in their own right, not just as symbols. This focus on, and respect for, the particular inevitably results in a more realistic and complex contrast between the two sets of perceptions than Plato's. The blind people have evolved an unusually acute sense of hearing and in this respect they must be reckoned the superiors of Nunez. Although Nunez descends into their world from above, like a visitor from heaven, their valley is situated in the mountains and he has previously had to ascend from a lower world.

Small as they may seem, these observations are enough to significantly change the tenor of the fable. We still side with Nunez in his attempts to convince the blind race there is an unseen reality since that reality is our own, yet the same truth discredits Nunez as an inspired law-giver. He is plainly no more a superman than any of us. On the contrary, his self-conceit and attempt to overcome the blind people by violence identify him as a potential tyrant.

Clearly 'The Country of the Blind' was not intended to be a story about the totalitarian implications of Plato's thought. It is about the plight of an isolated and thwarted visionary in a society which denies the truth of his revelation – in short, of someone very like Wells himself. (Nunez's conformist, blind sweetheart corresponds to Wells's first wife.) The precipitate behaviour of Nunez is included chiefly to make the shattering of his optimism more dramatic. Nevertheless an intuitive mistrust of absolutist thinking is built into the very texture of Wells's story, and this is characteristic of his work. Wells challenges normality by confronting it with a variety of testing fantasies adapted from the mythology of Christianity and Plato, but he challenges the absolute basis of those myths in turn by presenting them realistically.

His literary models for this double-edged satire again came from the Uppark library: *Gulliver's Travels*, *Candide* and *Rasselas*. In these books Swift, Voltaire and Samuel Johnson update the traditional marvellous voyage into an ironic quest. Though each of their travellers encounters a utopia, none can achieve a satisfactory conclusion to his journey. After fleeing the Happy Valley because life there seems aimless, Rasselas can only reach 'a Conclusion in which Nothing is Concluded'. Candide's extravagant misfortunes are relieved by his stay in Eldorado, but love and restlessness irresistably lure him away. Gulliver is deported from the Land of the Houyhnhnms because he is not a purely rational creature. Restored to human society but unfitted for it by his alien ideal, he adopts a comically misanthropic way of life scarcely distinct from madness. In an enlightened age when science and knowledge of other cultures have shaken up old certainties, true salvation proves impossible to find.

On a personal level Wells's scepticism evidently owed something to the influence of Uncle Williams, the phoney headmaster for whom he briefly worked. A Dickensian grotesque, complete with a hook for a hand, which unscrewed at meal-times to be replaced by a knife, Williams had a style of 'facetious scepticism' (*EA* Ch. 3:5) which greatly impressed his young relative – so much so that he seems to have used Williams with his chin 'like the toe of a hygenic slipper' as the model for the satirical rogue Chaffery in *Love and Mr Lewisham* (Ch. 11).

However, the main source of Wells's scepticism is likely to have been still more personal: his rapid movement through the social order, which would have made the biases of different groups stand out especially clearly to him. In the opening passage of *Tono-Bungay* George Ponderevo, very much a surrogate for Wells, observes,

> Most people in this world seem to live "in character;" they have a beginning, a middle and an end, and the three are congruous one with another and true to the rules of their type [. . . .] They have a class, they have a place, they know what is becoming in them and what is due to them, and their proper size of tombstone tells at last how properly they have played the part. But there is also another kind of life that is not so much living as a miscellaneous tasting of life. One gets hit by some unusual transverse force, one is jerked out of one's stratum and lives crosswise for the rest of the time, and, as it were, in a succession of samples. That has been my lot, and that is what has set me at last writing something in the nature of a novel. (Ch. 1:1)

Looking at Victorian England from outside in a 'succession of samples', Wells could see many of its assumptions being overthrown by the growth of knowledge and the repercussions of new technology, as in the controversies over Darwin's theory of evolution, which challenged accepted distinctions between man and animal, and the emergence of the socialist movement, which challenged man's division by class. Society's efforts to assimilate the sceptical observer to itself by forcing him into a tombstone-worthy 'character' would have done little to reconcile him to orthodox thinking. Indeed his unwelcome classification as a draper may have had a lot to do with his lifelong suspicion of all categories.

In time Wells elaborated that suspicion into a philosophy which he opposed to both Christian and Platonic absolutism. Since no two persons, objects or events could be completely identical, our ideas about them could only be roughly accurate, he reasoned, generally applicable but liable to fail in awkward cases. This was partly a way to excuse his own eccentric practices – literary, sexual or otherwise – when they were called into question. He could always think of himself as a special case, an exception to the rules. Unfortunately, extreme nominalism is an entirely negative philosophy, while what had been needed above all else by Wells when he was an unwilling drapery assistant, anxious to deny his given place in society, was a positive scheme of thought which could draw anything and everything into a satisfying pattern, legitimise his ambitions, guide his actions. Without faith in the supernatural or in some kind of absolute, where was he going to look for salvation? The answer lay in those popular encyclopedias to which he now turned: science.

In science Wells found a perspective that could make the commonplace reality which hemmed him in look frail and provincial. It offered new, exciting ways of looking at the familiar world and revealed hidden patterns of which that world was indisputably part. In these respects the atheistic *Freethinker* had been a disappointment. He says, 'It left me altogether at a loss for some general statement of my relation to the stars' (*EA* Ch. 4:2). At Uppark he discovered and assembled a piece of scientific equipment, a telescope, and as he was later to write, 'made my first contact with the starry heavens in a state of exaltation.' (*EA* Ch. 3:7). To him these magnified stars were not mere data, but a vision through which he could feel himself lifted up out of the everyday and united with the cosmos. The experience may have prompted his later adaptation of a biblical figure for triumph into an emblem featured in several of his books: a child standing on the earth as upon a footstool, laughing and reaching out its hands amid the stars.

This posture suggests something more than contemplation. Having purged established beliefs and made clear the true laws of nature, science then lets us turn those laws to our advantage. Once seen from the new viewpoint, the world is open to change. The nineteenth century was the century when, to many, science seemed capable of changing almost everything, and Wells was someone who wanted almost everything changed. With a science scholarship as his ticket to a better life he had special reason to associate science with the liberation of mankind.

Nor was he alone in adopting such an attitude. Many nineteenth-century thinkers assumed that science, having shown religious myths to be untrue, would go on to supplant religion more fully by delivering a replacement set of values. As the authority of God became less intimidating, the obvious course seemed to be to substitute the authority of science. In particular Darwin's work on evolution was used to justify a startlingly wide range of approaches to ethics and politics – individualism, Marxism, imperialism, nationalism, *laissez-faire* capitalism, racism – each of which, by applying the 'survival of the fittest' idea in a different way, appeared to vindicate its own peculiar presuppositions. Such thinkers overlooked the inconvenient fact that the laws which scientists identify and employ are laws of nature, categorically distinct from human laws of right and wrong.[3] Science tells us only what can be done, not what we ought to do.

In his first year as a student at South Kensington, Wells followed the biology course of T. H. Huxley. Huxley had, among many notable achievements, written an introduction to the philosopher who classically stated the above point, David Hume. Huxley accordingly insists in his famous 'Evolution and Ethics' lecture that ethical progress is not to be achieved by imitating the cosmic process, but by combating it.[4]

This insistence that man should stand on his own two feet still leaves the question, from where do we get our sense of right and wrong if neither God nor nature will supply us with guidance? Huxley's answer is that our ethical sense has evolved from the 'sympathy' creatures feel for others of their kind. As a survival trait for the group, 'sympathy' naturally flourishes in the individual.

Neat as this solution may be, its implications are very corrosive for human morale. It reveals ethical beliefs to be accidental in origin, liable to inconsistencies, at war with man's other animal instincts and variable from culture to culture. Without some standard of transcendent love beyond the present world of conflicting interests and constricting circumstances, how can any such thing as 'ethical progress' be established? Worse, if nature consists entirely of interlocking material processes, as scientists seem able to assume, then the ethical sense, along with all other mental activities, may be no more than a powerless by-product of the physical world. Symptomatically Huxley was prepared to entertain the notion that human beings are conscious machines, their thought no more in control of their actions than the smoke from a factory chimney is in control of what the factory produces.[5] In Huxley's secular view man becomes a fleeting gleam of consciousness, created, contained and finally extinguished by impersonal natural processes.

It was in direct response to this view that another great Victorian championed the study of literature as part of the curriculum. According to Matthew Arnold, the best that had been thought and said in the world would supply a humane perspective to complement scientific knowledge. Whether Wells was much influenced by Arnold is open to doubt (though he would later voice a wish to 'correct the estrangement between knowledge and beauty', echoing Arnold's wish 'to establish a relation between the new conceptions, and our instinct for beauty'[6]). It was presumably a parallel reaction to Arnold's, however, that led Wells after his first year as a student to ostentatiously neglect his scientific studies for literary pursuits and take on the pose of a 'philosophical desperado', challenging various beliefs of his day (*EA* Ch. 5:4). Wells himself came to blame his deviance on poor teaching in the second- and third-year courses. If so, other students were remarkably unaffected by it. The truth seems to have been that without the cosmic frame of reference Huxley brought to it, science lost much of its appeal for Wells. Instead of textbooks on physics and geology he preferred to read the writer and artist William Blake, who contemptuously dismisses the scientific world view of his day and contrasts it with his own imaginative apocalyptic vision.

Wells always enjoyed drawing comical 'picshuas'; one of 1886 shows him surrounded by manuscripts entitled, with half-guilty irony, 'How I Could Save the World', 'Whole Duty of Man', 'Key to Politics', 'Wells Design for a New Framework for Society' and 'All About God' (MacKenzie, illustration 12). These titles are very un-Huxleyite but very Wellsian. They are ones to which the young cartoonist would eventually fit real books.

None of this is to say that Wells consciously rejected science as a vehicle of salvation. His early science fiction does show that he saw the difficulties of Huxley's standpoint, but in his efforts to break free of his origins his own identity had become indissolubly bound up with the idea of science as a revolutionary world view. Even if in some respects science seemed to discredit the ideal, in other respects it still offered him his only hope that the ideal could be realised.

The dilemma is expressed in two articles he composed at the beginning of his literary career, 'The Universe Rigid' and 'The Rediscovery of the Unique'.[7] The former tries to imagine complete objectivity. Seen from a notional point outside space and time, it argues, the universe would appear as a closed material system, frozen and unalterable, with no place in it for the ideal. In 'The Rediscovery of the Unique' Wells seeks a way out through experiment. Since no one has access to a standpoint beyond space and time, no one is in a position to say how events are going to develop. Therefore people are entitled to believe that the future they desire may yet come about, taking heart from the nominalist assertion that in a universe composed of unique and so finally unpredictable objects anything might be possible.

This use of extreme scepticism to rationalise extreme credulity has affinities with the pragmatic philosophy of William James, whom Wells later befriended through his brother, the novelist Henry James. William James argues that if religious belief has an immediate value in keeping up the individual's morale, then where truth cannot be known the best response is not the agnosticism of Huxley. The individual may make a leap of faith. Wells principally differs from James in his elimination of the supernatural. He wants an end to the suffering and uncertainty of mankind in this world, in the foreseeable future, and through human resolution, not divine intervention.

In a short article of 1896, 'Human Evolution, an Artificial Process' (*Early Writings* pp. 211–19), Wells suggests that the moral progess of civilisation which once came from the biblical prophets now comes from 'eccentric and innovating people' such as novelists and journalists who challenge the established order. Their ideas may in time be translated into a perfect social order by 'men with a trained reason and a sounder science'. The formidable alliance between artist and scientist might eventually create a world where every creature would be happy – a wish which recalls the forecasts of the prophet Isaiah rather than Huxley's thinking. Yet Wells is sufficiently mindful of Huxley not to expect science to design his utopia, only to build it. Never at any stage of his life did Wells claim that the goals he put forward were guaranteed to be correct by science. What he did do, however, was assume they were especially compatible with it, which in practice can easily amount to the same thing.

In his 'Human Evolution' article Wells is still in the Arnoldian phase. It is to literature he looks for a vision of the ideal. Later he came to see literature as just one component, often a faulty component, in an emerging collective mind made up of all that is soundest in human culture. The concept of a 'Mind of the Race' offered Wells reassurance that the goals he put forward had more rightness and coherence than the speculations of one individual could hope to possess, yet did so without quite evoking an absolute authority. Even when he personifies the Mind of the Race in *God the Invisible King*, Wells clearly distinguishes this god from the one he rebelled against as a child. He is not 'God the Creator' but 'God the Redeemer'. He is not responsible for the universe and for the conflict and suffering which it contains. On the contrary, he represents man's struggle with nature.

In pursuit of Wells's completed world view we have in this chapter soared some way beyond the physically weak, but spiritually resolute, young man who from modest premises in Woking began to unleash his compelling fictions upon the world. This young Wells was not a philosopher but an entertainer, a spinner of tall stories with an imagination of extraordinary power, a flair for lively comedy and a hungry bank account. His challenging ideas, half-formed and tentative, were subsumed in stories whose first aim must necessarily be to please. Even as late as 'Scepticism of the Instrument' (a 1903 lecture to the Oxford Philosophical Society, reprinted in *A Modern Utopia*) Wells concludes that, rather than some utopian paradise, our sense of humour and our sense of beauty are the best substitutes we are likely to find for 'salvation from the original sin of our intellectual instrument' in an 'uncertain and fluctuating world of unique appearances'. In the fiction of his first period, similarly, the apocalyptic ideas which swarm in his imagination are employed to shape and animate fundamentally sceptical stories.

The little known but entertaining *Wonderful Visit* shows this especially clearly. Its principal characters, a vicar and an angel, stand for the actual and the ideal. The Vicar is a Christian whose world view has been discredited by science and whose youthful good intentions have been eroded by complicity in an unjust society, yet who has never properly admitted either of these unwelcome truths to himself. The Angel, whom the Vicar mistakes for a rare bird and shoots down, proves to be the inhabitant of another dimension of existence which we glimpse imperfectly through reverie, dreams and myth. In effect the Angel incarnates the Vicar's lapsed idealism and his adventures serve to expose the absurdities and hypocrisies of the Vicar's world.

Free from many of our normal preconceptions, and naïvely benevolent in disposition, the Angel functions as a kind of *ingénu* like Gulliver, Candide or Rasselas. His puzzled attempts to come to terms with the world, together with the Vicar's comically painful attempts to explain it, afford plenty of opportunities for satire. But the humour cuts both ways, for the Angel is in conflict not only with the injustices of our society, which we might perhaps correct, but the natural suffering of a Darwinian cosmos where creatures must compete with and prey on each other. His moral vision is too radical to be achieved. Instead he himself becomes contaminated by our disagreeable reality. As a spontaneous land-socialist, he loses his temper with a bullying landowner, thrashes him with his own whip and leaves him for dead.

At the end of the book a housemaid whom, to the horror of her 'superiors,' the Angel has treated as an equal, throws herself into a fire at the vicarage to salvage his violin. Roused from his disillusionment by the example of her love, the Angel follows her and the couple are consumed or, in an ambiguous image of liberation and defeat, translated to the Land of Dreams. The only witnesses of their ascent are two representatives of the unfettered imagination, an idiot boy and a little girl. It seems for a while as if the girl may be going to follow the couple heavenward when she begins to wilt in a pretty manner recalling Dickensian children such as Little Nell and Paul Dombey. However, a repulsively knowing materialist, Dr Crump, is able to cure her by administering a fattening diet, and it is the Vicar who closes the story by dying, terminally demoralised by the irreconcilable conflict between his ideal and reality.

Only one character succeeds in demonstrating an alternative way of life, the so-called Philosophical Tramp. His spirited denunciations of the entire social order as a process of unnatural selection, which produces people without minds of their own, suggests the need for massive institutional change. Yet he drops out of society altogether, achieving a negative freedom solely for himself.

His response – apparently reminiscent of the life style Wells's father and brother Frank adopted once Mrs Wells had departed for Uppark – is a partially convincing one, since *The Wonderful Visit* does not suggest our world could ever be like the Land of Dreams. On the contrary, in the deaths of the Angel and the Maid, virtue and love seem to be consigned to a realm of mere sentiment. The burning vicarage in which they perish seems to blazon the failure of humanism, which has not found a sanction to replace the supernatural.

Such an allegorical interpretation fits the book, yet remains a trifle misleading. Wells is not constructing an argument but a playful story, meant to appeal primarily to the imagination and the sense of humour. His comic exuberance outweighs the implicit pessimism. The power of his satirical tone depends on the assumption that reforms are possible in the real, imperfect world. The fantastic ideal world, the Land of Dreams, is not a myth on the literal truth of which our ideals rely for their validity, but an entertaining fictional device. *The Wonderful Visit* is designed to make us laugh and make us think for ourselves. Like all Wells's books, it would have had to be banned from a utopia like Plato's as a subversive document.

3

Dissolving Views:
The Short Stories

Most of Wells's short stories were written in the first ten years of his career. Considering that they were principally intended to be diverting anecdotes, and that the marvels of science on which a number of them are based have inevitably dated, it is remarkable how many of them still retain their power. Five of the most outstanding are 'The Country of the Blind', to which we have already given some attention, 'The Door in the Wall', which will be discussed in the last chapter, 'The Star', 'Under the Knife' and 'The Man Who Could Work Miracles.' It is no accident that these stories are ones which focus Wells's deepest concerns particularly sharply.

In 'Under the Knife' the tension between the world views of science and Christianity shows up at its strongest. A biological perspective is evident early on:

> The higher emotions, the moral feelings, even the subtle unselfishness of love, are evolved from the elemental desires and fears of the simple animal: they are the harness in which man's mental freedom goes.

The anonymous narrator who suggests this is awaiting surgery. Throughout his illness he has been emotionally drained, a state which characteristically he attributes to his physical condition. Even his lifelong tendency to be unemotional could, he speculates, have a similar basis. All about him the natural world is stirring with spring; his own organism remains depressed.

When he sees a black barge towed along the Regent's Park

Canal by a 'gaunt white horse', we are expected to recall the ideas not now of science, but the Bible:

> And I looked, and behold a pale horse: and his name that sat on him was Death, and Hell followed with them. (Revelation 6:8)

These chilling words come from the last, most visionary book of the Bible, which foresees the final overthrow of death and the establishment of the New Jerusalem. Falling asleep in the park, Wells's narrator has a partly horrific, partly comic dream of the resurrection – gory bodies bursting through the ground like seeds come to life – which prefigures the regenerative events of his story.

They commence with his operation when, although chloroformed, he finds himself conscious and able to see into the minds of his doctors. The doctors accidentally sever a vein and the patient is released from the material world, entering what psychical researchers call an out-of-body experience.

Wells renders credible the existence of a mind independent of a brain by two techniques of which he was master: highly circumstantial description and the plausible matching of fantastic events to contemporary knowledge. It seems logical enough that, free of material inertia, the narrator should remain stationary while body, room, building, city, country, planet, solar system, even the stars, fall away beneath him. He becomes a detached point of consciousness, watching the world of humanity recede further and further – a situation which takes his cool, scientific view of life to its ultimate extreme. At first he feels liberated and serene but eventually, as the disorientation and loneliness of this detached existence overwhelm him, he experiences 'a passionate resurgence of sympathy and social desire'.

> The covering of the body, the covering of matter had been torn from me, and the hallucinations of companionship and security. Everything was black and silent. I had ceased to be. I was nothing.

As if to assure the narrator that human companionship with its foundation of natural 'sympathy', is not after all something

makeshift, but a reality endorsed by a supernatural order, the
entire universe dwindles to a speck on the ring of a giant hand.[8]
The hand is accompanied by a series of apparitions and a voice
says, 'There will be no more pain.' This declaration is adapted
from one at Revelation 21:4 which precedes the descent from
heaven of the New Jerusalem. In 'Under the Knife' it is the
ordinary world which is restored, altered only to the extent that
the narrator's own outlook has changed.

The vision resolves itself into his room, the various miraculous
signs corresponding to its contents. The voice becomes that of
the surgeon. On waking, the narrator finds himself cured of his
depression, but whether by surgery or divine intervention
remains unrevealed. The story does justice to the mystery of
experience by leaving the events capable of a materialist or a
spiritualist interpretation. Wells's own preference is implied
only in the narrator's earlier anticlimactic dream of the
resurrection, where the voice crying 'Awake!' turned out not to
belong to the Angel Gabriel but to a deckchair attendant
demanding payment.

'Under the Knife' places perennially compelling imagery
from myth and dream into a detailed, realistic picture of the
world with a skill equal to its audacity. The metaphysical
questions raised add to the story's power because they are
firmly embodied in its events, not left as abstractions. Like *The
Wonderful Visit*, 'Under the Knife' generates implications rather
than conclusions. It presents highly charged symbols, not
arguments. In this and much else it is in fact typical of the bulk
of Wells's short stories.

The great majority of them show a conflict between the
everyday and some other, more exotic world, the eruption of
the unexpected suggesting the precariousness of what currently
passes for reality. Wells introduces these eruptions in an
impressive variety of ways, skilfully locating them in realistic
settings and tracing their origins to one of several areas as yet
unconquered by science, where the usual rules may not apply:
space ('The Star', 'The Crystal Egg'), the ocean ('In the Abyss',
'The Sea Raiders'), the jungle ('The Flowering of the Strange
Orchid', 'The Empire of the Ants'), the spirit world ('The
Magic Shop', 'The Inexperienced Ghost'), revolutionary new
discoveries or inventions ('The New Accelerator', 'The Land
Ironclads'), drugged states ('The Purple Pileus', 'The Story of

the Late Mr Elvesham') and even the depths of the mind ('Under the Knife', 'The Door in the Wall').

At the point where the two worlds clash we often find an outsider figure taking the force of the impact, someone who, like Wells himself, is already at odds with society's consensus on reality to a degree. Nunez in 'The Country of the Blind' is 'a reader of books in an original way' who has travelled far beyond his native community; the narrator of 'Under the Knife' regards the world with extreme scientific detachment. In Wells's very best stories the fantastic events in which such people become involved dramatise their existing alienation and take it to a revealing new extreme. Nunez is altogether separated from the local people and the possibility of ordinary domestic happiness among them by his knowledge of the world beyond; the scientific observer becomes totally detached from the natural world. For them it becomes impossible either to accept ordinary life or find happiness anywhere outside it.

Some outsiders become fixated by a glimpse of the fantastic at once precious and tormenting. In 'The Apple' and 'A Dream of Armageddon' a luckless narrator has to share a train compartment with such a figure who, like the Ancient Mariner, verbally recreates his revelation and draws the listener into his obsession. In 'The Crystal Egg' a young scientist is engrossed by the case of a shopkeeper named Mr Cave (presumably with reference to Plato's parable) who escapes from commercial pressures and his bullying family by furtively peering into a mysterious crystal in which he can see the landscape of Mars. After Cave's death the scientist is left conducting a possibly hopeless quest for the vanished crystal.

The visions which Wells's short stories disclose are very much left open to interpretation by the reader, who may construe them mythologically, psychologically, sociologically and so on. Later in his career Wells would force a narrower interpretation onto such material. Already, however, it is clear that his use of symbols differs significantly from the general symbolist tendency in nineteenth- and twentieth-century Western art, where an openly non-rational creation of meaning defies the mechanistic world view associated with science.[9] While at first Wells may seem to set the realistic and the symbolic in opposition, the fantasies with which he conjures are not intended as an alternative to realism but an imaginative extension of it. It is implied that ultimately science will be able to absorb the fantastic into its secular, factual account of things. Wells's stories are strong in the sense of wonder; they convey only a token sense of the inhuman or the sacred. In three slyly blasphemous stories of man-made objects being mistaken for gods ('The Lord of the Dynamos', 'Jimmy Goggles, the God' and 'In the Abyss') characters who misinterpret the unfamiliar as the divine are implicitly ridiculed. Religion, Wells suggests, results from a failure of the primitive myth-making mentality to understand the real, material world.

Patrick Parrinder has noted a characteristic Wellsian motif in the last of these three tales, that of the lens or window (Parrinder pp. 36–8). He links it to Wells's use of the microscope as a science student; we may also link it to Wells's discovery of that telescope at Uppark. The presence of some kind of lens between the observer and the observed draws attention to the difficulty of interpreting the alien worlds which become juxtaposed with our own, and also suggests that if we could somehow enter those worlds with our wits about us we might be able to look back on our old reality from a startling new perspective.

Importantly related to this motif is the 'dissolving views' comparison used in 'The Story of the late Mr Elvesham' and 'The Remarkable Case of Davidson's Eyes'. Dissolving views, invented early in the nineteenth century, was a kind of slide show where lights behind sliding painted glass plates were brightened and dimmed alternately to dissolve one picture into the next. Its thematic relevance is that in each change of view there was a moment when the new image and the old were equally visible, but the new image could not yet be made out because it was still unfamiliar. While lenses suggest a perplexing glimpse of the unknown, the dissolving views comparison implies a historic progression from a known past to a knowable future. Our perplexity may be only a first reaction to something which is destined to grow clearer to us. In the opening chapter of *Tono-Bungay* Wells explicitly applies the dissolving views analogy to the shift in outlook between the Victorian and Edwardian eras. Like the image of intersecting gyres or cones used by his contemporary, the poet W. B. Yeats, it symbolises life in a period of transition, suggesting that a new relationship with the universe hovers just beyond our grasp.

It is deceptively easy to think of Wells and Yeats as complete opposites – the irreverent publicist of scientific progress versus the aloof and reactionary Romantic – but Yeats too had been led away from Christianity by the writings of T. H. Huxley, had sought new inspiration in the writings of William Blake and longed for the apocalyptic arrival of a new age. In an imaginary dialogue between the two authors Graham Hough seems to imply that Wells was pedestrianly literal-minded in his use of apocalyptic symbolism compared to the great Irish poet, but in fact both applied their ideas with an uncertain mixture of literalist belligerence and self-mocking irony.[10] Yeats' desire for a new order could become sufficiently crude and immediate for him to sympathise with Fascism, while Wells with paradoxical integrity preached elitism to the masses and criticised the failings of every elite he encountered, Fascist, Communist, Catholic, even Fabian.

Yeats defied the secularity of science by believing in a spirit world, while Wells was implacably hostile to superstition. (The spirits who do appear in some of his stories are a feeble, sub-human bunch, tending to caricature and usually rationalisable as part of a fourth dimension which science will one day explain.) Yet Wells ultimately found that he did require something like a utopian religion based on the Mind of the Race. His early work shows why. The adoption of a Huxleyite scientific perspective all too often results in exactly the view of man from which Yeats was trying to escape. People are reduced to the status of objects or animals, scurrying through a grubby world, doomed by forces they cannot control, unenlightened by love or any workable system of ideals, driven only by a blind Darwinian desire to survive. Any knowledge of science they possess is liable to constitute a threat rather than an asset.

In 'The Lord of the Dynamos', for example, the engineer Holroyd, who 'doubted the existence of the deity but accepted Carnot's cycle', metaphorically sacrifices a savage to the machine they both tend, only to be literally sacrificed to it in return. The primitive struggle for survival and dominance which underlies human behaviour is laid bare in 'The Reconciliation' and 'The Cone', both of which depict men fighting to the death over a woman. The climax of 'The Cone' comes when a husband pushes his wife's lover into a furnace.

> His human likeness departed from him. When the
> momentary red had passed, Horrocks saw a charred,
> blackened figure, its head streaked with blood [. . . .] a
> cindery animal, an inhuman, monstrous creature that began
> a sobbing intermittent shriek.

The pathetic animality of the victim and the brutal passion of
his assailant disclose the nasty truth beneath the surface of
civilisation. In 'The Empire of the Ants' and 'The Sea Raiders'
the human race finds itself being drawn into single-minded
competition with another species which implicitly dethrones
man from his unique position as overlord of nature (an idea
Wells develops with maximum devastation in *The War of the
Worlds*), though perhaps we should also be thinking here of the
afflictions mankind has to suffer in Revelation before the
millenium can begin.

All these tendencies are outstandingly exemplified in 'The
Star', a work in which Wells's imagination is given the chance
to operate at full stretch and rises fairly splendidly to the
occasion. The challenge to complacency in this tale comes from
the collision of a wandering planet and Neptune. First evidence
of the cosmic upheaval is visible only through telescopes, but it
is not long before the incandescent mass begins to grow and
dominate the skies for all to see. As the 'star' comes closer and
encroaches on everyday reality, panic sets in. People are forced
to realise that the conditions they once thought fixed are
nothing of the sort. Geological history speeds up around them.

> And upon all the mountains of the earth the snow and ice
> began to melt that night, and all the rivers coming out of
> high country flowed thick and turbid, and soon – in their
> upper reaches – with swirling trees and the bodies of beasts
> and men.

Note the binding together of 'beasts and men', equal in their
powerlessness when faced with the new conditions, alike reduced
to objects borne along at the whim of a suddenly plastic reality.
Note also how Wells typically seizes on the logical consequences
of the fantastic – if the temperature rises, ice will melt and
floods flow – increasing the plausibility and vividness of the
story. (Note also the slightly clumsy syntax: a repetition of

'flowed' is understood after the second dash, but the word is positioned a little too far off to take effect. This carelessness is also typical.)

By juxtaposing many particular experiences of the catastrophe, Wells is able to build up a global montage adequate to the scale of the action. The rapid cutting from scene to scene precludes the emergence of an outsider figure at the very centre of the story, but a master mathematician, the first person to comprehend what is happening, does find in his perception of mankind's approaching death a confirmation of his own uncommon identity.

'The Star' was first published in the Christmas issue of the *Graphic*, 1897. Given this context, and its rather biblical phraseology, it can be seen to parody the gospel story of a star shining to herald the birth of Jesus. Instead of signalling God's goodwill to man, Wells's star signals the indifference of nature. To some extent the story is not just an imaginative but a satirical vision, an iconoclastic joke at Christendom's expense, displaying what Joseph Conrad called Wells's 'cold jocular ferocity' (quoted Parrinder p. 39). Satire necessarily implies some positive standpoint and Wells supplies this when, after the upheaval has ceased, the survivors join together in a 'new brotherhood'. Presumably they have found in the disaster a common experience powerful enough to unite them into a real global community. The challenge of nature has succeeded where the preaching of religion failed. Ironically the star does usher in an era of peace after all.

Yet, in one of those imaginative *coups* which make Wells's early work so enjoyably unpredictable, the last paragraph of the story takes the narrative standpoint further back than ever, putting events into still another perspective. To Martian astronomers, we are told, earth's transformation is chiefly remarkable for its slightness.

> Which only shows how small the vastest of human catastrophes may seem, at a distance of a few million miles.

The story ends as it began, with sightings from observatories, the lens motif quietly insinuating the partiality of all standpoints.

The reference to a 'new brotherhood' in 'The Star' is an uncharacteristically utopian gesture. Most of Wells's short stories take on any larger significance they may possess in a subtler way, through their symbolic implications, which are usually highly destructive. Positive values are less likely to be transmitted through the events of the story than through the voice which narrates them.

The Wellsian narrator manages to get a reassuringly steady view of a world of melting certainties by his scrupulous attention to factual detail and his evident respect for the power of science, if not for those who clumsily unleash it. His emotional response to the disruption of the normal world is consistently one of enjoyment. For the reader too, fantasy converts even the most horrific events into tall tales which can be taken in with undisturbed pleasure, while the frequent practice of narrating at a remove (referring back to some apocryphal document or the testimony of a fictitious character) helps encourage detachment. Ease of assimilation is further aided by the assertive, lively style of presentation Wells had developed in his articles and reviews, a cheerful, improvisatory manner ever liable to break off in a string of dots.

It may be helpful to digress here briefly on Wells's use of language. It is an aspect of his work often passed over in silence by critics, and with some justification Wells is prime evidence for George Orwell's dictum that good prose is like a windowpane.[11] To update the image, we may say that his words are like lines on a television screen or pixels on a VDU, there to carry the information, not to be seen in their own right. That Wells's writing can be slapdash is not necessarily relevant. It is meant (changing the comparison again) to be bolted greedily, with only the occasional phrase or passage relished for itself. One particularly memorable example of such a passage is the description of Chester Coote's cough in *Kipps*,

> a sound rather more like a very, very old sheep a quarter of a mile away being blown to pieces by a small charge of gunpowder than anything else in the world. (Book II, Ch. 8:3)

The parodies of Henry James's style in *Boon* are a rare instance of sustained verbal invention. Wells's work is more often enlivened by the use of slang and phonetic spelling in dialogue. 'Poggit-handkerchief, quig!' demands a drapery customer ('A

Catastrophe'). 'SUZANNA! 'ETS! SUZANNA! 'ETS!' a twenty-first century hat advertisement proclaims in upmarket Cockney, ''ets r chip t'de' ('A Story of the Days to Come'). With phonetic spelling goes onomatopoeia, as in the intriguing opening of 'A Vision of Judgment,' 'Bru-a-a-a.'

Sometimes Wells adopts a contrastingly weighty tone. This imparts a prose-poem quality to 'The Star', but is more usually applied to commonplace subjects for droll effect. Both strategies should be distinguished from reliance on words such as 'whither', 'thrice', 'betimes' and inversions such as 'it troubled me not' to impart a literary colouring, though these in turn are to be distinguished from certain archaic forms which Wells habitually and neutrally prefers to more modern usages: 'over against' for 'opposite', 'darkling' for 'dark', 'save' for 'except', 'rare' for 'occasional'. Considering his style was formed in the 1890s, Wells is remarkably free of such Victorian usages, having taken, in his own words, 'a cleansing course of Swift and Sterne' (Preface to Atlantic Edition, Vol. I). The remark is suggestive. Wells escapes the ponderousness of much nineteenth- and early twentieth-century literature, not by moving towards the self-consciously experimental styles and forms of the Modernists, but by reviving the clarity, detachment and narrative freedom he had found in Defoe, Swift and Voltaire.

A particularly extreme example of these features being used to brightly package horrendous material is 'The Man Who Could Work Miracles', a comic variation on the Midas theme in which practically all life on earth is violently destroyed. The story seizes happily on the incongruity between the other worldly gift of working miracles and the unshakeably mundane character of its recipient, Fotheringay, whose wishes at first rise no higher than a 'miraculous new tooth-brush'. Mr Maydig, a local church minister, has grander ideas. He persuades Fotheringay to re-enact a biblical miracle, the halting of the moon (Joshuah 10:12), with a token and, as it proves, unfortunate concession to scientific knowledge. Instead of stopping the moon directly, Fotheringay stops the rotation of the earth. Naturally the cataclysm which ensues destroys everything on the earth's surface.

Fotheringay narrowly manages to save his own life and, having done so, brings the universe to a halt while he thinks over the situation. He decides to restore everything to the way it was at the beginning of the story, then deprive himself of his miracle-working ability. Even his own memory of his adventures is cancelled. Those present fail to notice the end of the world. Only the reader and Wells see, from their privileged position, that normality rests on conditions which at any moment may turn out to have been precarious.

If this tidy restoration of the old reality, with the threat observed from a secure, congenial present, is characteristic, so is the equivocal implication. To try to master the deeper forces of nature is highly dangerous; yet, as we are so vulnerable to natural disturbances, perhaps we should be pursuing science far more urgently. Both of these paradoxes are, as we shall see, central to the early scientific romances.

4

The Mark of the Beast:
The Early Science Fiction

The term 'scientific romance' is a good indicator of what the books it describes contain. Like the more recent 'science fiction' it yokes together two apparent opposites: science and art, knowledge and fantasy. In Wells's scientific romances, man is both a questing spirit trying to break through the barriers of material reality and an imperfectly intelligent animal shaped by the forces of nature. The heroic spirit seizes on the power of science as a means to free itself, but as the consequences of Wells's 'impossible hypothesis' are explored (*Literary Criticism* p. 241), finds itself disappointed or even deconstructed into a terrifying bestiality. Robert P. Weeks has claimed that disentanglement from an imprisoning reality, followed by exhilaration, then disillusionment or defeat, is the basic plot behind all Wells's fiction (*Critical Essays* pp. 25–31). It informs his non-fictional writings too. Nowhere, however, is it more intensely expressed than in *The Time Machine*. Into this, his first book-length story, Wells poured ideas and obsessions he had nursed for years, working over the text again and again till it rang true.[12]

The Time Traveller is the prototypical Wellsian hero, defying established notions of reality for a greater one revealed through science. In the opening pages of the book he intrigues and disconcerts a group of guests to his house, the narrator among them, by challenging their notions of space-time. Priding ourselves on grasping his meaning more readily than these minor characters do, we become, without realising it, Wells's true victims, for we are lured into making an imaginative investment in the idea of time travel and so begin to be drawn into the vision to which it will lead.

The Time Traveller is a kind of modern prophet who aims to transcend the mundane, not by receiving a revelation from God, but by taking advantage of a secular fourth dimension to examine man's destiny at first hand. For Wells and the reader, the fourth dimension is the imagination informed by science; in the world of the book, it becomes a perplexing and dangerous voyage into the future which belittles ordinary existence and robs the Traveller of his bearings.

> I saw great and splendid architecture rising above me, more massive than any buildings of our own time, and yet, as it seemed, built of glimmer and mist. (Ch. 4)

Light and dark – traditional symbols of knowledge and ignorance, and good and evil – merge into a grey flux. Committing himself to a new standpoint too abruptly, the Traveller tumbles headfirst into a 'pitiless' grey hailstorm, out of which looms an ominously eroded sphinx-like figure, representing the riddle of what his experiences may signify.

At first the Traveller seems to have discovered a secular heaven: a green and pleasant landscape dotted with exotic structures and peopled by an apparently carefree race. Wells's model for this may have been the Botanical Gardens at Kew, with its greenhouses, pagoda and holidaymakers, located a few miles from the Traveller's home in Richmond. The Traveller describes the future world as a 'garden' – also T. H. Huxley's epitome for the precarious State of Art which man develops out of the State of Nature – and imagines himself to have reached the concluding, pastoral stage of a William Morris-style communist utopia.[13] He soon finds the 'utopia' to be less than ideal. If mankind has freed itself from suffering and conflict, it is only at the cost of degeneration. The 'utopians' may have a kind of beauty but they are also puny and unintelligent. The Traveller reasons that in a secure world there is no demand for strength or intelligence, and that under these circumstances natural selection will therefore, contrary to expectation, bring about degeneration.

Some doubt is cast upon his ingenious theorising when he finds his vehicle has been dragged into the sphinx by unknown forces. The journey through the fourth dimension has not after all made the course of human development completely clear or placed him outside its problems. He feels suddenly cut off from any shared reality, like 'a strange animal in an unknown world' (Ch. 7), a sensation of being completely trapped which is the exact reverse of the desire to range at will through time with which he set off. Dismayed, he tries to force passers-by to reveal the secret of the sphinx, but they react with horror to his questioning of a taboo subject, a response frustratingly similar to the incomprehension and derision of his Victorian contemporaries.

Mutual sympathy with a fellow creature is re-established and with it the possibility of ethical behaviour, when he rescues Weena, one of the future 'people', from drowning. But he has to admit that even she may have seemed 'more human than she was' (Ch. 11) and his fear of finding a race 'inhuman, unsympathetic' (Ch. 4) is fulfilled when he discovers his time machine has not been taken by Weena's people, the Eloi, but the subterranean Morlocks. (The clumsy introduction of the two names is the one flaw in an otherwise scrupulously written book.)

The name of these heirs of evil aptly recalls Moloch, the biblical term for infanticide, generally taken to be the name of a false god to which Israelite children were sacrificed. The word Eloi appears prominently in the New Testament when Jesus cries out on the cross,

> Eloi, Eloi, lama sabachthani? which is, being interpreted, My God, My God, why hast thou forsaken me? (Mark 15:34)

Beneath the innocent-seeming paradise of the witless Eloi lurks a godless reality in which the nocturnal Morlocks await the coming of the night, when they will be able to emerge and exercise their power.

As several critics have noted, the fantastic set-up recalls the actual world of Uppark, where the servants' areas were located below ground-level, giving the young Wells an unusually diagrammatic view of the class system at work. There were ventilation holes to the lower level, as shafts connect the worlds of the Eloi and the Morlocks. Like the Time Traveller, Wells was a visitor who found the social system he saw grotesque and beyond self-correction. As he grew older, he looked for a third class, of rebels like himself, to emerge in the world outside, which he saw as essentially analogous to Uppark. This elite could take power from the moribund aristocracy and try to remake as many of the lower class as possible in its own progressive image. *The Time Machine* depicts the consequence if this revolutionary class should fail to appear. The aristocrats (Eloi) and labourers (Morlocks) have devolved into the lesser creatures they deserve to be. Revolution can now occur only in parody form. The human race has split into two as often foretold (they indeed resemble the prophesied opposites, capitalists and workers, saved and damned), but the new world they inhabit is a savage mockery of the ill-conceived promises of Marxism and Christianity, and the docile, vegetarian Eloi, once the masters of the carniverous Morlocks, have now become their meat supply.

The Traveller's defiant descent into the underworld of the Morlocks resembles, it has been suggested, the Harrowing of Hell by Christ (Bergonzi pp. 52–3). The Traveller had already taken on the appearance of a messiah figure at his first meeting with the Eloi, humouring their naïve idea that he had come down to them out of the sky. However, trapped in a parody of the apocalypse, he is unable to free the Eloi and lead them to salvation.

The Traveller's possession of matches does establish a limited superiority to those around him. He is a representative of science, able to manipulate the forces of nature. But what the matches illuminate when he gets beneath the deceptive surface of the world is a ruthless exploitation of creature by creature which compromises man beyond any possibility of redemption. Concluding 'The Rediscovery of the Unique', Wells had written:

> Science is a match that man has just got alight. He thought he was in a room – in moments of devotion a temple – that his light would be reflected from and display walls inscribed with wonderful secrets and pillars carved with philosophical systems wrought into harmony. It is a curious sensation, now that the preliminary splutter is over, and the flame burns up clear, to see his hands lit and just a glimpse of himself and the patch he stands on visible, and around him, in place of all that human comfort and beauty he anticipated – darkness still. (*Early Writings* pp. 22–31)

When the matches the Traveller strikes reveal horror and cause destruction, he reveals himself to be part of a universe to which ideas of heaven and hell are finally irrelevant: one formed out of material processes, from which human values and aspirations emerge as mere by-products. What is implicit in the thinking of T. H. Huxley becomes concrete in the Time Traveller's adventures. Any independence from the material world humanity may have achieved does not open the way to transcendence, but to a painful and irreconcilable tension between the actual and the ideal.

A derelict museum the Traveller visits exhibits that no object is permanent or value absolute. Exuberantly exploring it, and making up a dance for Weena out of the various long-lost dances he remembers, the Traveller finds a trivial but satisfying use for man's heritage. However, this post-cultural play is short-lived. After the couple leave they are set upon by the Morlocks and the camphor the Traveller has salvaged from the museum becomes the source of an all-consuming fire which kills Weena.

Even while he is stumbling through the man-made hell of the fire, violently beating off the Morlocks, the Traveller clings to his faith that there is still some way of transcending the material and the bestial. The stars glimpsed through the smoke symbolise liberation, as they once did for Wells at Uppark. The Traveller feels he is caught in a nightmare; he calls upon God to awaken him.

Faith sustains him in the struggle to escape and recapture the time machine, but a fresh immersion in the fourth dimension leads only to a still more distant future when all sign of the human race has disappeared. Perched alone on a wintry beach, he gazes at the bleak seascape from which life once emerged, and into which, reversing the process, vegetation and giant crabs are now returning, oblivious to the claims of Genesis and Revelation. The eclipse of the sun which first startles, then demoralises, the Traveller brings the light and dark imagery of the story to a climax with darkness entirely dominant. Fortunately the sun is not actually extinguished. The fear of being eaten by some residual predator is enough to drive the Traveller back onto the machine and to the safety of the 1890s, a period when degeneracy and the *fin de siècle* are fashionable ideas, not yet unbearable realities (Bergonzi, pp. 1–14 and 60–1). His experience of the world's end seems the conclusion of the story, but at this point neither he nor Wells has completed his mission. The revelation has still to be related to the late-Victorian world from which the voyage began.

The Traveller's guests reject his news of the future with the same unimaginative complacency they brought to his theory of the fourth dimension. Again this encourages the reader to take the vision comparatively seriously, and construe it in a way critical of their assumptions. The Traveller's call for meat, plus a reference to servants at his house, indicate that the horrific system of exploitation revealed in the future is continuous with the natural and social inequities of the present. If its inhabitants could see it from the standpoint of a time traveller, or a philosophical desperado, they might even discover Victorian Richmond itself to be a type of hell.

With his sense of what is real and what is acceptable disturbed, the Traveller makes an anguished exclamation which recalls those of the ideal-tormented Vicar in *The Wonderful Visit*.

> They say life is a dream, a precious poor dream at times – but I can't stand another that won't fit. It's madness. And where did the dream come from? (Ch. 16)

One way to cope with such a disintegrating world view might be to do as the Philosophical Tramp: withdraw from the social consensus into an outlook based entirely on your personal convenience. Significantly the Traveller's guests liken his ill-used appearance to that of a tramp or a beggar. Up until the Great War, Wells often displays a sentimental attachment to Romantic vagrancy as an alternative to the commitment of the revolutionary.

The Time Machine does not, however, end with advice on how to live, what to do. Instead the exploratory story is completed by an ambiguous image. Our last glimpse of the Traveller is of a practically invisible man as he returns into the fourth dimension, never to reappear. This image brings the themes of disorientation, alienation and devolution to an appropriate end. Having seen through everything, the Traveller dissolves too. Yet his return into the fourth dimension also affirms that dimension's reality, as Robert Philmus has pointed out (*Critical Essays* pp. 67–8). By embracing annihilation the Traveller demonstrates his allegiance to a perspective greater than his time- and space-ridden contemporaries dare acknowledge. As when the Angel throws himself into the burning vicarage in *The Wonderful Visit* and Nunez returns to the mountains in 'The Country of the Blind', self-fulfilment and self-destruction combine.

The Traveller's disappearance is still not quite enough to conclude the book, so the narrator comes forward with a brief commentary, stressing the problematic nature of his friend's revelation and making a cautious commitment of his own to the day-to-day struggle to revise and extend our civilisation. His commitment exists in open tension with the Traveller's reported scepticism, but is too low-key and stoical to be undermined by even the most powerful vision of ultimate failure.

> He, I know – for the question has been discussed among us long before the Time Machine was made – thought but cheerlessly of the Advancement of Mankind, and saw in the growing pile of civilisation only a foolish heaping that must inevitably fall back upon and destroy its makers in the end. If that is so, it remains for us to live as though it were not so. ('Epilogue')

Sympathy, such as that shared by the Traveller and Weena, can at least generate temporary meaning. The book's final, equivocal image is of two flowers given to the Traveller by Weena and brought to our era, flowers which have now, in the course of time, shrivelled and died.

If the Traveller stands for the liberated imagination stimulated by the perspectives of material and social science, then the narrator, whose voice contains and filters the Traveller's, represents the part of ourselves which has to get down to the business of everyday living. The presence of the narrator, even at its most token, stops us becoming so involved with the Traveller's adventures that we are overwhelmed by their implications or, as is more likely, that we retreat into a thoughtless incredulity. Instead we are encouraged to adopt the attitude the Traveller requests from his fellow Victorians.

> Take it as a lie – or a prophecy. Say I dreamed it in the workshop. Consider I have been speculating upon the destinies of our race, until I have hatched this fiction. Treat

my assertion of its truth as a mere stroke of art to enhance its interest. And taking it as a story, what do you think of it? (Ch. 16)

The challenge draws attention to the playful quality of all Wells's earlier fiction, which makes its primary appeal as entertainment and resists over-literal interpretation. When the Traveller breaks free of his era he does not attain a god's-eye view which shows him a new certainty; he launches himself into perpetual exploration. No matter how demanding and distressing this exploration proves for him, the requirement that an adventure story will include sudden, shocking developments pleasingly contains the horror and perplexity for the reader. Analysed by critics, *The Time Machine* may be, as some have called it, desolating; simply read, however, it is enormous fun. The fantastic form the Traveller's adventures take ensures they do not affect us as would kinds of suffering we might share. Even the references to meat and servants, which suggest a moral connection from the fantastic to the real, are placed before the account of the journey itself, severely diminishing their effect.

If Wells did not play down the story's implications in this way the Traveller would become a tragic figure, but this is a strictly forbidden development in Wells's fiction. Wells's rebels against the social consensus are never allowed to be discredited unless they are clearly weak, wrong-headed characters like the Vicar in *The Wonderful Visit* whom we are not intended to take seriously. The Angel, with whom we identify to a far greater extent, though he may have to die to this world, succeeds in defying it at the same time by making contact with an alternative outer world, the Land of Dreams. The Time Traveller and Nunez are each in a similar position, lifted above pathos by their experience of a greater reality. This is also how Wells seems to have seen himself in his early years – an outsider, doomed by ill-health, a failure by the world's standards, yet the forerunner of a new age which would sooner or later break apart the stuffy, ignoble world around him.

The autobiographical connection is a little more explicit in his second scientific romance, *The Island of Doctor Moreau*, since like Wells its protagonist-narrator Edward Prendick is a former student of T. H. Huxley. His adventures are a grisly illustration of Huxley's belief that the State of Nature tends always to subvert man's State of Art, from without and from within. *Doctor Moreau* has never quite achieved the popular esteem of *The Time Machine*. To the casual reader it may seem rather gratuitously and obsessively macabre after the varied moods of its predecessor, but it must still be accounted a remarkable piece of work.

It begins with a shipwreck which establishes the fragility of civilised behaviour when put to the test. With the provisions in their dinghy exhausted, Prendick and two other survivors are driven to try cannibalism. The others topple overboard in a struggle for survival; Prendick is picked up by a passing ship, but not restored to the world of human sympathy. His rescuer, Montgomery, insists that the decision to save him was purely a matter of chance. It seems that if Montgomery had any deliberate motive it was merely a ghoulish curiosity to find out whether Prendick had eaten any of his fellow passengers. The squalor aboard the ship, fittingly named the 'Ipecacuanha' (after a medicine which induces vomiting), shows life at its most degraded.

When the ship reaches the tropical island for which Montgomery is bound, the drunken and malicious captain casts Prendick adrift. Montgomery saves him once more but his motivation is again suspect since Prendick's training as a biologist makes him potentially useful as an assistant for the owner of the island, Doctor Moreau.

All the early scientific romances have an appropriately 'scientific' structure, with theories formulated and discarded as the evidence is pieced together, until the real truth appears. In this case, after several guesses from Prendick about the situation on the island, it becomes apparent that Moreau is engaged in a secret attempt to turn beasts into people by a pioneering combination of 'spare part' surgery, drugs and hypnotism. Moreau's account of his project, largely lifted from Wells's science journalism (compare Ch. 14 and *Early Writings* pp. 36–9 and 194–9), offers a disturbing view of human nature, the more so in that many of the ideas it contains no longer sound quite so far-fetched as they must have done in the 1890s: religious emotion is based on sublimated sexuality, the principal difference between man and monkey is that the monkey's larynx cannot create a sophisticated language.

While Moreau's doctrines challenge the traditional view of man as God's special creation distinct from the animals, his actions burlesque Christian mythology in a way comparable to William Blake's parody of Genesis, *The Book of Urizen*. Moreau once worked on the creation of an ape man for a week, then rested. He also made a murderous serpent creature. Setting free a number of rabbits on the island, Montgomery offers them the ironic blessing, 'Increase and multiply [. . . .] Hitherto we've had a certain lack of meat here' (Ch. 6), adapting theology to biology.

The objects of Moreau's experiments, the Beast People, worship him in a vain attempt to appease his wrath and preserve their woefully unstable human qualities. The traditional view of humanity is one of a divine spirit corrupted by the body, but the Beast People are animals corrupted by an impossible ideal. Their Law, which they are constantly chanting and constantly breaking, parodies the reactionary laws which Kipling had projected onto nature in his recently published *Jungle Books*. More generally it satirises human hypocrisy, for the deepest impulse behind the Beast People's religion is not love of virtue but fear, fear that the most powerful being in their cosmos will return them for modification to his laboratory, their equivalent of hell. As befits a personification of the cosmic process, Moreau is indifferent to their suffering and incapable of saving them.

The idea that an ethic could be consciously founded on sympathy instead of fear is given equally satirical treatment. Hearing a puma being vivisected in the room next to his, Prendick realises he is more concerned that the distressing noise should stop than that the suffering itself should be relieved. This leads him to reflect that the simple existence of others' suffering does not trouble us, only its presentation to our senses. And even that can be inconstant. Fleeing back to Moreau's building from a series of frightening adventures, Prendick hears the puma's moaning with some relief. Next morning, after Moreau has again been at work on the creature, the puma's cry becomes that of a woman. This shocking substitution confronts us dramatically with the question whether there is any real boundary between the sufferings a human being and a beast experience.

Moreau is not a merely demonic figure. His goal is a heroic one, to create a more rational race, less subject to their physical sensations. Pleasure and pain are, he claims, 'the mark of the beast', to be transcended (Ch. 14). The phrase 'the mark of the beast' is taken from Revelation where a mark set on the right hand or forehead identifies the opponents of Christianity in the Last Days. Yet, since it is Moreau who rules over the Beast People, the term seems to identify him as an Antichrist figure. When Moreau leads the Beast People in the hunting down of the regressing Leopard Man, Prendick realises the pursuit is not a rejection of animality at all but a crude and nasty sublimation of the hunting instinct. Moreau's supposedly transcendent allegiance to scientific progress, overlooking as it does Huxley's distinction between the ethical progress of humanity and the mere cosmic process of nature, can result in nothing but unusual varieties of bestiality.

Prendick speaks of the mark of the beast again towards the end of the book when, after the death of Moreau, the Beast People regress with ever greater rapidity. Wanting to hold back this degeneration, Prendick is forced to take on the role of prophet, assuring the Beast People that Moreau has ascended into the sky and will return one day to punish those who have broken the Law in his absence. This resort to religion to control the Beast People satirises its use as a tool of class oppression, but Prendick's observation that 'it takes a real man to tell a lie' (Ch. 21) is also a way of saying that what crucially distinguishes man from the animals is precisely his capacity to create and manipulate myths, establishing a shared sense of reality and rectitude. While Prendick's desperate attempts to play the role of prophet mock Christianity as a mythology which has become incredible and inadequate to the discerning mind, there is a serious implication that an efficient mythology of some kind may still be necessary for civilisation.

Some of the Beast People claim they can follow the Law without the Moreau myth, but in the end rational commitment proves powerless to control their animal impulses. Traditional religion and Romantic humanism join each other on the scrapheap. Both deny man's essential animality and suppose the existence of a spirit or noble savage beneath the surface, which can be redeemed by being cleansed of worldly corruption.

Wells dissents from this view, but gives an equally dualistic, Jekyll-and-Hyde account of human nature in his article 'Human Evolution, an Artificial Process'.

> In this view, what we call Morality becomes the padding of suggested emotional habits necessary to keep the round Palaeolithic savage in the square hole of the civilised state. And Sin is the conflict of the two factors – as I have tried to convey in my *Island of Doctor Moreau*. (*Early Writings* p. 217)

Deprived of such cultural reinforcement, the irrational and egotistical impulses of the savage take over, as in the case of Montgomery whose affinity to the Beast People finally draws him into a drunken rampage with them, culminating in his death.

Prendick alone continues to exercise self-control. Just as he declines to endorse Moreau's evolutionary mysticism or the simple-minded Law of the Beast People, so he refuses Montgomery's offers of alcohol, proclaiming himself a lifelong abstainer. However, this puritanical guardianship of his human integrity does not prevent him being compromised by the disintegrating culture about him more subtly. In resisting the temptation to act like Montgomery, he shows a lack of sympathy for him all the more reprehensible since Montgomery has twice saved his life.

That he treats the Beast People with still less sympathy is to be expected; but when at long last Prendick is rescued and taken back to civilisation his mistrust of the Beast People is reapplied to mankind. Having interpreted the situation on the island as a microcosm of the human condition, he now finds it impossible to distinguish between the human beings produced by evolution and the travesty of them produced by Moreau.

> I could not persuade myself that the men and women I met were not also another, still passably human, Beast People, animals half-wrought into the outward image of human souls, and that they would presently begin to revert, to show first this bestial mark and then that. (Ch. 22)

Prendick's descriptions of civilised man contain some satirical exaggeration ('the preacher gibbered Big Thinks even as the Ape Man had done'), but rest on a view of nature which has been demonstrated and expounded throughout the book. The only resistance to it comes from within Prendick himself. He would be greatly relieved to find a convincing view that was more heartening. Indeed he claims to have already begun to do this with advice from a mental specialist. But his withdrawal into a world of books, chemical experiments and the contemplation of the stars through a telescope, founded on a regard for the 'vast and eternal laws of matter', differs from Moreau's approach only in its greater passivity and sentimentality.

As Wells's apocalyptic visions increasingly take a form relevant to the actual world, and their greater length entails a more open development of their significance, the very credibility of the view that mankind is the doomed victim of uncontrollable forces demands a counterbalancing utopian view be spelled out, so that Wells is unable to reproduce the simple poise achieved in 'Under the Knife' or *The Time Machine*. Apocalyptic despair, on the one hand, and apocalyptic idealism, on the other, loom up in obvious but often unacknowledged tension.

In *The Island of Doctor Moreau* the conflict is not yet sufficiently obvious to cause damage. The utopian ideal is largely channelled into the contemporary article, 'Human Evolution, an Artificial Process,' while the romance itself makes an entertaining, coolly satirical use of mythology. Wells's chief model here is Book IV of *Gulliver's Travels* which carefully skirts the whole idea of religious transcendence and leaves man placed between two fabulous creatures, the completely rational Houyhnhnms and the completely bestial Yahoos, in both of whose natures he seems to partake. Wells's Beast People are literary descendants of the Yahoos, while Moreau discredits pure rationality as a way to human salvation. Like Swift, Wells leaves us in part amusing, part disturbing suspense.

The third of the scientific romances, *The Invisible Man*, has more obvious entertainment value than *Moreau*. Its central character is another scientist who wants to change the world, but he is no idealist. His adventures amount to a less complex, more melodramatic story where bizarre situations are exploited in turn for thrills and comedy. However, the fate of the mad scientist Griffin does still dramatise the question whether scientific knowledge and the power it brings are ultimately compatible with human sympathy.

Griffin tries to use invisibility to turn himself into a dictator presiding over a reign of terror, but his squalid, unidealistic goal leaves him rather unimpressive. At times he does become sinister and frightening, but at others he is pathetic, even comic. From the first his idea that science will set him free proves false. After a painful and spectacular transformation scene, he steps out into the world exultantly, only to find himself stumbling, colliding with people, being chilled by the weather, hurt by rough ground, chased by a dog, given away by his footprints and unable to eat in public. He is able to get back into society only by constructing a temporary public self with items stolen from a theatrical costumier, as a 'swathed and bandaged caricature of a man' (Ch. 23) rather like one of Moreau's Beast People. Having become an invisible man he is no less conspicuous than he was formerly as an albino. He does not even manage to die with the heroic bearing of a tragic figure, but calling out for mercy with his last breath from beneath a mob.

Griffin's revolt against the injustice, ugliness and 'sordid commercialism' of society goes with a 'loss of sympathy' (Ch. 20) which prevents him developing his rebellion beyond a vicious self-assertion; yet there is something moving in his fierce determination to defeat a mean world and his attempts to do so are indisputably exciting. Like the disembodiment of the Time Traveller as he slips into the fourth dimension, the invisibility of Griffin expresses a terrible alienation from normality but also an appealingly vigorous defiance of its constrictions.

After Griffin's death his body gradually reappears. Its creeping visibility is likened to 'the slow spreading of a poison' (Ch. 28), a comparison previously used to describe the contamination by mortal life of the Angel in *The Wonderful Visit* (Ch. 50). More directly it recalls Griffin's use of the poison strychnine as a tonic. Another character in the book, Kemp, calls strychnine 'the palaeolithic in a bottle' (Ch. 20), identifying its use as a surrender to the baser element of man's nature.

Kemp was once a fellow student of Griffin's. His distaste for strychnine is equivalent to the abstinence from alcohol of Prendick, and he resembles Prendick too in being a Good Scientist with a responsible attitude, brought in as a foil to the

Bad Scientist. Yet, rather more explicitly than Prendick, he is implicated in the unhealthy world view he opposes. Early in our acquaintance with Kemp we see him gazing up at the stars in reverie, speculating about the social conditions of the future and about the time dimension. This readiness to take on startling new points of view marks his mental kinship with Griffin, who had also turned to stare at the stars when he first realised that he might make himself invisible.

Griffin mentions this incident after a bullet wound has forced him to take refuge in Kemp's house. Griffin's retrospective account of his adventures, which explain the mysteries of the first part of the book and prepare us for the conclusion to come, do something to draw us in to his point of view, but his outbursts of callousness and Kemp's interjections qualify our sympathy. However, we must regard Kemp ambivalently too, for his hostility to Griffin seems to be based less on superior morality than on his superior position in the social order. While the brilliant Griffin is a shabby demonstrator at a provincial college, Kemp is respected and secure. He has a large house, servants and a private income. He shows no understanding of the outcast and is equally ruthless. When he offers Griffin a chair it is not out of genuine concern but in order to place him where he cannot see the police coming.

Kemp's betrayal of Griffin, and abuse of his confidences when giving the police advice on how to harass him, arouse our sympathy for the fugitive. This in turn is dispelled by news that Griffin broke a child's ankle as he fled from Kemp's house. The events of the story are carefully balanced so that we are unsure whether to regard Griffin as inhuman or afflicted, hateful or pitiful. Although Griffin's own attacks on society are crude and unsuccessful, Wells's development of their implications calls into question some of the categorisations society employs.

After the threat of Griffin has been ended by his death the books containing the secret of invisibility are left in the hands of a comical tramp he bullied into assisting him, Mr Marvel. As his name suggests, he is a kind of alternative to the marvellous Invisible Man. Marvel too rejects society's demands on him, but not by enacting violent fantasies. With what remains of Griffin's stolen wealth he opens a pub called the Invisible Man which, in parallel to Wells's activity as author, enables him to trade on the sinister story of the Invisible Man while keeping

his own grip on human sympathy. Meanwhile the scientist
Kemp also desires to possess the books and we are left uneasily
aware of the threat new knowledge may yet pose to an
unprepared world.

That world is altogether transformed by the knowledge and
power of science in *The War of the Worlds*, Wells's most
outstanding combination of documentary technique and
hallucinatory vision. Griffin had visited mere slapstick
destruction on the village of Iping, but the Martians subject the
entire Home Counties to a monstrous assault. 'I had expected
to see Sheen in ruins,' reflects the narrator, ' – I found about
me the landscape, weird and lurid, of another planet' (Bk II,
Ch. 6).

The anonymous speaker is a scientific observer in the mould
of Kemp and Prendick, and again it is the implications of his
own world view which are brought so spectacularly to light. A
prosperous writer on philosophical themes, he is occupying
himself when the book opens by speculating on the probable
development of moral ideas with the progress of civilisation and
by learning to ride the bicycle. Ironically the Martians who are
about to descend on his world are more 'advanced' than
mankind and – emerging from their space cylinders to attack
London from giant tripods, using heat rays and poison gas –
they apply technology to what from our point of view seem
totally destructive ends.

Science may enable the narrator to loftily contemplate the
stars through a telescope, but the extension of awareness opens
up a disorientating, relativistic view of the universe. The
narrator's inspection of Mars through a telescope is preceded
by the complementary image of the Martians looking down at
us as through a microscope, locking us in an uncomfortable
position somewhere between the Martians above and microscopic
organisms below. Among those organisms are the bacteria
which will destroy the apparently invincible Martians after our
own defences have humiliatingly failed.

The narrator celebrates the bacteria (to which we, unlike the
Martians, have a natural resistance) as God's humblest creatures
and declares with a pompous recourse to biblical diction,

By the toll of a billion deaths, man has bought his birthright

of the earth [. . . .] For neither do men live nor die in vain
(Bk II, Ch. 8)

His pronouncements recall similar remarks on the will of God in
Defoe's *Journal of the Plague Year*, one of Wells's models, but in
Wells's book pious observations have a hollow sound. After all,
the explanation of the Martians' failure is persuasive because it
deals solely with material causation, while his assumption that
God takes an active interest in the survival of the human race
carries little weight in the light of God's apparent indifference
to individual human suffering and to the survival of the
Martians, who must also be His creations.

The effective world view of the book is of a universe in which
good and evil are relative, depending on your ecological
position. In *Evolution and Ethics* Huxley had pointed out that a
gardener does not maintain his garden by sympathising with
weeds, slugs and birds, but by keeping them down. When the
Martians drop out of the sky to replace mankind as earth's
dominant species, they naturally take over our role as gardener
while we become the undesirable slugs. The narrator of *The War
of the Worlds* repeatedly compares the Martians' treatment of
human beings to the way modern man has treated both animals
and the 'inferior' races within his own species.

> The Tasmanians, in spite of their human likeness, were
> entirely swept out of existence in a war of extermination
> waged by European immigrants, in a space of fifty years. Are
> we such apostles of mercy to complain if the Martians warred
> in the same spirit? (Bk I, Ch. 1)

As Martian supplants man, it becomes evident that their
monstrosity only mirrors our own.

Since the motive for their invasion seems to be that Mars is
becoming infertile through age, the journey through space to
our younger world is also a kind of journey through time, which
shows us what our descendants may become through natural
selection. The Martians even resemble a forecast of the man of
the future made in 1893 by a 'certain speculative writer of
quasi-scientific repute' (Bk II, Ch. 2). (The writer was, needless
to say, Wells himself. The article, 'The Man of the Year

Million', is collected in *Certain Personal Matters*, retitled 'Of a Book Unwritten.') The narrator explains that the development of the brains and hands at the expense of the rest of the body might have resulted in the Martians' present octopus-like form and suggests that this would be accompanied by a loss of their 'emotional substratum'.

From this it appears that values are not only relative but ultimately dispensable. There is a subtle resemblance between the Martians, 'intellects vast and cool and unsympathetic' (Bk I, Ch. 1) who have evolved beyond humanity, and the little child who, not yet fully socialised, watches a man being crushed to death 'with all a child's want of sympathetic imagination' (Bk I, Ch. 16). While trapped in a ruined house the narrator reflects on how deeply human values depend on material processes. He peers out at the Martians' activities and sees robots working and reproducing themselves without supervision – perhaps the next stage of evolution. When the vampiric Martians set about their meal of living people with a 'sustained and cheerful hooting' (Bk II, Ch. 3), the word 'cheerful' makes an unexpected appeal to our sympathy which invites us beyond the stock response to them as mere monsters.

The narrator is equally at odds with our expectations of a hero, for his observation that men and Martians follow similar principles of behaviour is confirmed whenever he finds himself under pressure. Sharing the ruined house with a deranged curate whose ravings eventually attract the Martians' attention, he clubs him with a meat chopper in a vain effort to silence him in time, turning back the blade with 'one last touch of humanity' (Bk II, Ch. 4). The Martians drag the curate out; the narrator survives as a victor in the struggle for existence. Earlier, to give his own wife a means of escape, he hires a small carriage from a pub landlord who does not yet know about the invasion. One creature is to survive at the expense of another, as in the Martians' appropriation of the earth. Although he does try to return the carriage, he finds the publican dead.

The narrator readily overcomes his feelings of guilt through prayer but, as previously noted, the book offers little encouragement to religion. The attempts of the curate to construe the invasion as a divine punishment only expose his feeble-mindedness. To his query, 'What are these Martians?' the narrator is forced to retort, 'What are we?' (Bk I, Ch. 13).

A more powerful diagnosis is put forward by an artilleryman who draws a vivid picture of the limitation and meanness of suburban life, welcomes the collapse of civilisation and proposes the formation of an underground elite which will adapt to the new conditions and learn from the example of the Martians. His vision is ingenious and exciting, but powered by ill will. It is shaped by a desire to take revenge on society for its disrespectful treatment of him in the past, which Wells (understandably, given his own background) enjoys expressing but still recognises to be unhealthy. The artilleryman's project of burrowing into the sewers is symbolic. The narrator abandons him when he realises his ideas are a self-serving fantasy which he will never put into practice.

This discrediting of the moral philosopher, the man of religion and the soldier stand for a general discrediting of mankind. Exposed to a greater reality, human culture breaks down. Many are killed in mindless panics. Wells writes of the police and railway organisations

> losing coherency, losing shape and efficiency, guttering, softening, running at last in that swift liquefaction of the social body. (Bk I, Ch. 16)

The image recalls the degeneration of Moreau's Beast People –

> Can you imagine language, once clear-cut and exact, softening and guttering, losing shape and import, becoming mere lumps of sound again? (Ch. 21)

– and also the view from the time machine:

> the whole surface of the earth seemed changed – melting and flowing under my eyes. (Ch. 4)

Seen in a moment of crisis, or from a sufficient conceptual distance, human existence is revealed as an aimless flux.

At the end of the book the old order is shakily restored after the Martians' chance defeat. The narrator is even reunited with his wife, but the reunion is a piece of formula writing that carries no conviction. Here, as in most of Wells's science fiction, personalities and personal relationships seem beside the point. *The War of the Worlds* is not a study of character in action. Instead it takes our anxiety about war and disaster, and develops it into a 'worst case' scenario using a logical pattern of events and vividly observed locations. The power of this tactic was classically illustrated by Orson Welles's notorious radio broadcast of 1938 which updated the invasion, located it in New Jersey and resulted in a mass panic among its listeners.[14] For those who do realise they are being told a story, it is the fantastic, extreme character of the events which permits them to be enjoyed, distancing the anxiety and transforming it temporarily into pleasure. For modern readers the close descriptions of the Home Counties at the turn of the last century add an element of nostalgia, further promoting the charm, lessening the fear.

Wells's science fiction always implants the fantastic in the real world with complete authority. Our imagination is won over by Wells the Novelist's gift for the plausible detail: the puffs of green smoke from the joints of the Martian tripods as they stride unhurriedly across the fields, the fading pigment of the Invisible Man's eyes hovering in his room as he looks through himself in the mirror. When the time comes for explanations, Wells the Science Journalist can always muster some equally plausible argument. Events follow from each other with seemingly impeccable logic, drawing us with them into a transformed world.

At the story's ending almost all is made well. Order is restored on the surface, yet the more thoughtful readers will have gathered that the previous disorder was not arbitrary. It briefly allowed us to see into things from a disturbing angle, even if Wells did not dwell on the implications glimpsed.

In the early scientific romances Wells uses the perspective he acquired through his social dislocation and science training as a means to challenge the existing world, not as a vision of life in its own right. He had not escaped the drapery by surrendering to a tragic view of mankind as the victim of irresistible forces. For him to make that perception more explicit, it would have to be contained by some contrary, utopian vision – a difficult task, but one to which Wells would devote himself over the next half century.

5

Pitiless Benevolence:
The Later Science Fiction
and Utopias

Postponing discussion of *When the Sleeper Wakes* for a moment, since it represents such a significant break with Wells's previous approach, we must consider *The First Men in the Moon*. This book is generally grouped with the early science fiction, but acknowledged to be a lesser achievement both in intensity and unity. It begins as a comic novel with Bedford, an opportunistic bankrupt, befriending an eccentric scientist, Cavor. The mood shifts to one of wonder as the two employ a gravity-repelling substance to fly to the moon. Under the lunar surface they discover an alien civilisation which furnishes an opportunity for social satire.

Their voyage takes place at the end of 1899, the year commonly reckoned to be the century's last. The story began serial publication in what was mathematically the last month of the nineteenth century, December 1900. Shortly after the explorers reach the moon they hear a booming from underground like 'the striking of some gigantic buried clock' (Ch. 10). The symbolism is clear enough. If the account of the hidden world from which this noise comes constitutes

> the first warning of such a change in human conditions as mankind has scarcely imagined heretofore (Ch. 24)

it is not only because interplanetary war may one day ensue. The lunar society also contains cryptic forecasts about our own civilisation's development in the coming century.

Wells seems to intend Bedford, who narrates the story, to be a representative of contemporary Western society's worst features. He shows little social responsibility or idealism, and his capitalism and imperialism are merely ways to sanction and organise selfishness. When he discovers that lunar gold is abundant and that low gravity gives an overwhelming physical advantage to Earthlings, he makes up his mind to claim the moon and sets about massacring the natives.

Cavor is less opportunistic, more creative. He has a healthily Spartan way of life and takes a more open minded attitude than Bedford towards the inhabitants of the moon, the Selenites. Yet he is also a comically limited figure, uninformed by a sound world view, ignorant of the arts, oblivious to the commercial and military implications of his work and, in his innocence, easily exploited both by Bedford and the Selenites' ruler, the Grand Lunar.

Cavor's name, like Cave's in 'The Crystal Egg,' recalls Plato's parable. After watching the lunar dawn from the window of his interplanetary sphere, he is able to go beyond the lens into the world revealed to him and discover there a quasi-utopian order, but it is one which will prove fatal to him. That Wells intends a reference to the parable of the cave, suggestive of frustrated enlightenment, is confirmed when Cavor and Bedford awaken as captives beneath the lunar surface, for they are bound in a dark, enclosed place, able to see only the outline of a Selenite cast on the far wall as it opens a door behind them.

Beyond the door they discover an efficient, stable civilisation based on the principle that each citizen should do solely the work for which he is judged fit. The principle is Plato's, but implemented in an unexpected way. Pursuing the ideal to its logical conclusion, the Selenites physically warp each new generation in order to make them fit the division of labour required by their social order, producing a race of swollen-headed administrators, musclebound policemen and hands who are merely that.

Wells's portrayal of this superefficient state as inhuman takes account of criticisms which T. H. Huxley had made of Plato's utopia.[15] Setting aside his own determinist speculations in order to combat collectivism, Huxley had argued that people are autonomous individuals who enter flexibly into co-operation on a basis of mutual sympathy. Ruthless regulation of them for a supposed collective good would destroy this sympathy and bring about social disintegration, especially when it was applied in the intimate world of the family. The kind of social cohesion envisaged by a thinker like Plato could apply only to a society where each individual was biologically predestined to fulfil a particular function, like that of the beehive. Wells's imaginary society of insect-like creatures seems to illustrate this argument.

However, while the Selenite practice of deforming their offspring caricatures the way that human individuals have been denied fulfilment by constricting social roles (Wells at the drapery among them, of course), our world is equally condemned for its failure to achieve an efficiency and cohesion like that of the Selenites' – qualities only made possible by the distortion. It is highly tempting, and not far from the truth, to accuse Wells of confusion. Strictly though, his position can be defended, for he is not offering us a pattern to imitate or oppose, but an imaginative challenge. Once more the double irony derives from *Gulliver's Travels*. This is clear when Cavor attempts to impress the Grand Lunar with accounts of life on earth only to expose its irrationality and evil, the same *faux pas* Gulliver committed before his Houyhnhnm master and the King of Brobdingnag.

In order to preserve its impressive cohesion the Selenite society has to guard itself against any disruptive influence from outside, by excluding humanity and fresh knowledge. At the end of the book Cavor reveals that he alone possesses the secret of space travel, and the Selenites drag him away, presumably to his death. Here too there is an awkward paradox, however. Without highly sophisticated science the Selenites would not have been able to develop themselves and their environment so as to achieve perfect stability. Can their static ideal be compatible with science as Huxley understood it: a force which would tend to erode arbitrary authority and increase freedom? Other people may take a more jaundiced view of science than Huxley, but they must still acknowledge its dynamic character, its propensity to transform society in unintended and seemingly irresistable ways. No one has been more aware of that powerful social effect than Wells, yet his Selenites show no awareness at all that science is a revolutionary force capable of exploding utopias from within. In his own utopias Wells would always try to allow for further scientific progress and consequent social change. Whether, once unleashed, change can so easily be allowed for and so tamely channelled may, however, be doubted.

The First Men in the Moon is principally concerned with the excitement of passing between a comic, realistic world of disorder and a sinister, fantastic one of rigid organisation, not with arguments about political idealism. However, in the context of Wells's writing as a whole, it is important that the mock-Platonic order is presented with a qualified respect. If the model cannot be applied to human beings directly, the possibility is left open that some modification of it might suit our needs. The human race must come to terms with the effects of science rapidly, as is clear from what happens when Cavor first creates his anti-gravity substance. A dispute about job demarcation among his labourers leads to an explosion which blows up the house and nearly blasts the earth's atmosphere into space. Such a disaster could not come about, we gather, in the futuristic society of the Selenites. When Cavor explains democracy to him the Grand Lunar responds by ordering cooling sprays on his brow, then asks for a repetition under the impression that he must have misunderstood.

On what basis could we create a better social system? Wells hints at his answer in an interlude when Bedford is returning to the earth alone. For no apparent reason the astronaut is transformed into a kind of 'cloudy megalomaniac' (Ch. 19) with an overwhelming sense of detachment, as if he had moved out of space and time entirely, allowing him to see his normal self and behaviour reduced to comically petty proportions. Here, although he does not know it, Bedford is getting a glimpse of what a man who wants to revolutionise the world most needs: a revelation. A standpoint outside space and time, which completely transcends individual partiality, would be the ideal one from which to construct a perfect society – if only such a standpoint existed.

The sort of sensation Bedford undergoes is a recurrent one in Wells's fiction.[16] (We have already seen something similar in 'Under the Knife'.) This suggests that in his crosswise movement through society Wells had had similar feelings of total detachment. Since he did not believe there was an absolute standpoint, he came to associate such feelings with the next best thing, the Mind of the Race, which would naturally be felt more and more in people's individual minds the nearer they got to the prospect of utopia.

It should be emphasised at this point that Wells's utopianism was not just a personal quirk. His desire to change the world no doubt took shape from his social mobility, and his growing optimism that change might be near was similarly related to the improved health, prosperity and status which came to him with the new century. However, his Edwardian works were also part of a general attempt by writers of fiction to advance from the kind of imaginative secession from contemporary reality which had dominated the 1890s to a new position of critical engagement.[17] It was because he was a particularly fluent spokesman for a general tendency that Wells's ventures into non-fiction had such encouraging public success.

The socialist critic Raymond Williams has defended Wells as a historically important writer on the grounds that he was especially sensitive to the real large-scale changes taking place in the world.[18] In this view the best of his scientific romances and novels have vitality because they imaginatively bypass the limiting attitudes and frames of reference found in more orthodox fiction, while the more tendentious works, which eventually became his standard output, fall short of success because in them he substitutes a naïve goal of world government for serious investigation of what is taking place. This account of Wells is a fair one so far as it goes, yet it gives a slightly limited view of what Wells was up to.

Certainly he was aware that the continuing industrial revolution demanded profound political changes, but he went further. Science was also demythologising our view of the universe, depriving us of any meaningful notion of our place in it. Wells's twentieth-century fiction has as one of its major aims the countering of that vision of meaningless flux present in his earlier work.

Wells expects the development of science to transform the world so radically that some complementary system of guiding ideas has just got to be produced.

The old local order has been broken up or is now being broken up all over the earth, and everywhere societies deliquesce, everywhere men are afloat amidst the wreckage of

their flooded conventions, and still tremendously unaware of
the thing that has happened [. . . .] no world-wide culture of
tolerance, no courteous admission of differences, no wider
understanding has yet replaced them.

Unfortunately, as the closed society of the Selenites suggests, a
'wider understanding' is sought by way of a myth which
actually tends to exclude the 'courteous admission of differences'.

In the *Modern Utopia* from which the above pronouncements
come (Ch. 2:2) Wells depicts only a limited area of toleration
within an authoritarian framework. A utopian religion
underwrites the social order. Its basis – the repudiation of
original sin – seems to contradict Wells's earlier contention that
man is fundamentally bestial and in need of regulation through
'suggested emotional habits' (*Early Writings* p. 217), but in fact
the new religion is included precisely to suggest such emotional
habits. Whether it really guarantees the integrity of the utopian
world view or is compatible with the findings of science does
not overly trouble Wells. Like Prendick on the island of Doctor
Moreau, he is too busy preaching to the potential beasts around
him to worry about lesser things. Wells is less of a hypocrite
than Prendick, however, since he attempts to convert himself
also.

There is a worse danger than incoherence in this sort of
preaching. Utopias take their shape from the prejudices of their
authors. To imagine a perfect future is necessarily to prejudge,
to take a short cut through the practical and moral problems
ahead. If the pretence of having solved these rationally is good
enough to fool the author himself, some of the most extreme
attitudes that his underlying anxieties and aggressions can
generate may manage to infiltrate the utopia. Wells had found
a better way to vent those negative feelings in *The War of the
Worlds*.

> I'm doing the dearest little serial for Pearson's new magazine
> in which I completely wreck and sack Woking – killing my
> neighbours in painful and eccentric ways – then proceed via
> Kingston and Richmond to London, which I sack, selecting
> South Kensington for feats of peculiar atrocity. (MacKenzie
> p. 113)

Within the book the temptation to make such feelings a guide to action is mocked by the example of the Artilleryman. In the utopian works, because Wells is trying to overcome the opposition between reality and desire, that kind of irony is no longer available. The consequent denial of ambiguity and ambivalence is accompanied by a tendency toward crude, messianic power fantasy.

The weakness is at its plainest in certain parts of *Anticipations*, Wells's first attempt at popular non-fiction. His forecasts are supposed to be based on historical analysis, but to Elizabeth Healey, the same friend who had received the above comments on *The War of the Worlds*, he admitted that *Anticipations* was a propaganda job

> designed to undermine and destroy the monarch, monogamy and respectability – and the British Empire, all under the guise of a speculation about motor cars and electrical heating. (MacKenzie p. 162)

Wells looks ahead to several generations of cultural disintegration, forming a period without general faith in any set of customs or ideals. An elite of technocrats finally emerges, capable of establishing a new order (the 'New Republic') consonant with a divine purpose the faithful find in the universe. Wells identifies himself with the elite and writes approvingly of a world where the penalty for being unlike him will be death or, if lesser punishments are retained, 'good scientifically caused pain' (Ch. 9). The ruling 'artists in reality' will have 'little pity and less benevolence' for lesser creatures because they will have 'an ideal that will make killing worth the while'. The New Republic's treatment of the bulk of the so-called 'inferior races' does not quite amount to formal genocide, but for those who fail to conform to its standard the end is not in doubt, 'they will have to go'.

Wells's utopianism had made a more modest debut in the 1897 novella 'A Story of the Days to Come'. This story depicts a future society which combines the worst of Selenite-type organisation with unregulated competition. It apparently represents a stage in the development of the totally unjust society to be reached in *The Time Machine*. As the upper and lower classes have not yet evolved into distinct species, there seems a possibility that a better order could still be created. The question is how. Wells merely offers a couple of hints. One of the central characters makes an inarticulate declaration of faith in mankind's destiny; a doctor brusquely remarks that scientists may eventually take power from the rich men and party bosses.

In *When the Sleeper Wakes* Wells revives this future society and imagines it being transformed for the better. Significantly, the revolution does not come from within the world depicted, but has to be crudely imposed from outside. Graham, a Victorian radical, wakes up from a two-century coma to find that the actions of the stock market have made him owner of the world. Like the Time Traveller, he explores the new society and lays bare a system of exploitation which he finds intensely distasteful, but from his uniquely priveleged position Graham has the opportunity to inspire and direct a revolution against it.

Unfortunately Wells's attempt to advance from creating parody messiahs like the Time Traveller to a true one is thwarted by lack of any convincing ideal for Graham to champion. Appeals back to Victorian values are doubly inadequate since Graham was tormented by the conflicts in Victorian society when it existed (overwork on political pamphleteering sent him into his recordbreaking coma!) and it was from the injustices of Victorian society that the vicious social order of the future developed. Graham's difficulty in establishing a standpoint is symbolised by his frequent ascents to high places from which the world can be regarded comprehensively, followed by desperate descents toward human commitment.

In itself Graham's disorientation does not spoil the book. He could have become a tragic figure, obliged by circumstances and his own sense of responsibility to fashion a precarious basis for action out of his perplexities. But Wells will not have half measures. Instead he sets the people of the future responding to Graham as a convincing messiah, modelling the story on those of Christ and the Emperor of the Last Days, the warrior-saviour who was paired with Christ in the messianic mythology of medieval Europe.[19] Graham's principal admirer, Helen Wotton, compares him to King Arthur and Barbarossa, describes his sleeping face as god-like and habitually refers to him as 'Master'. He is tempted in a high place, quotes from St

John's gospel and in Chapter 8 undergoes a kind of symbolic crucifixion. In the revised version of 1910 he urges his followers to surrender themselves to faith 'as I would give myself – as Christ gave himself upon the cross' (Ch. 23). The role of Antichrist is taken by a demagogue, Ostrog, whose savage colonial troops are equivalent to the hosts of Gog and Magog traditionally fought by the Emperor of the Last Days. Graham refers to the coming battle with them as 'Armageddon'; Helen declares, 'We have God on our side' (Ch. 23).

Since the book predates Wells's Mind of the Race speculations, the god to which Graham turns is a kind of afterimage of the Christian deity, invoked from despair rather than faith. Nor does Graham's championship of the common people carry much conviction since Wells consistently depicts them as the mindless rabble they have been declared to be by Ostrog. In a preface added in 1921, shortly before he joined the Labour Party, Wells tries to allegorise the myth, making the Sleeper

> the average man, who owns everything – did he but choose to take hold of his possessions [. . . .]

Yet a benevolent dictator makes a poor symbol for the average. If Graham represents anything, it is surely the abrupt, inexplicable emergence of a collective will.

Wells's principal achievement in *When the Sleeper Wakes* is his influential conception of the future city. The comparative plausibility of the city discredits the plot played out there. While Wells tries to persuade the reader that Graham is the agent of a better order, he actually shows him fleeing from the confusing world of today into one where issues can be confronted in a simplified form. This impression is reinforced by the ease with which Graham secures almost universal adulation from the citizens of the future, contrasting with the failure of his marriage in his own era.

The basic myth is dramatically undercut, however, when it comes to the book's conclusion. Instead of supplying Graham with victory over Ostrog, followed by the establishment of a perfect world, Wells leaves the outcome of the conflict uncertain, with Graham plunging to his death in a damaged aircraft. By disappointing apocalyptic expectations Wells restores the uncertainty of real experience and, with it, the individual responsibility of the reader. Yet the shocking conclusion is also a way of evading the implications of apocalypse, without any awkward need to show the kind of society that would result from it. To the unwary, Graham's decision to die fighting for a better world rather than to thrive as puppet-ruler of Ostrog's regime may look like a rejection of egotism. In fact Graham's solo combat with a fleet of aircraft and his death before an adoring audience are invitations to project self-admiration and self-pity.

Wells recognised that *When the Sleeper Wakes* was unsatisfactory. His next scientific romance, *The First Men in the Moon*, is, as we have seen, much warier in its treatment of utopianism. He even revised the former book as *The Sleeper Awakes*. Unfortunately the removal of some discursive passages and of the conditional tense from the title show a determination to make the book more assertive, rather than any perception that its major flaw lies in irrational closure. This is representative of the trend of Wells's thought.

In *The Food of the Gods*, for example, he tries to crudely symbolise the power of science – initially disruptive, finally therapeutic – through a growth-inducing drug. Realistic presentation subverts his intention. The enlarged wild creatures in the first part of the book are convincingly frightening. The idea that the giant children in the second part represent an improvement on normal human beings is not supported by any evidence. It is simply the self-interested opinion of the giants and the scientists responsible for their creation.

A far more successful attempt to show things changed for the better is made in *In the Days of the Comet* where realism and fantasy are carefully partitioned. The first part of the book is a novel narrated by a young office-clerk named Willie Leadford, presenting conflict between individuals, social classes and nations. The second half is a romance in which all of these are overcome when a comet discharges a sanity-inducing gas into the earth's atmosphere. The realistic and fantastic elements are not allowed to conflict so openly this time, but again Wells's metaphor is inadequate to sustain the burden placed on it and his vision of reconstruction remains less than persuasive. If the disappearance of the various conflicts does carry some conviction, it is really because they are seen shallowly both before and after the transformation, through the eyes of a rebellious teenager, and because the new world is a matter of millenarian symbols rather than utopian plans.

In his socialist study *New Worlds for Old* Wells admits that the vision of *In the Days of the Comet* has no practical application. The same could be said of all his attempts to picture a perfect world, as a vision of perfection can be kept free of ironies only by making its connections with reality critical and oblique. The very word 'utopia' embodies the problem. Sir Thomas More coined it in his *Utopia* of 1516 as a descriptive pun on the Greek 'eu-topos', meaning 'good place', and 'ou-topos', 'no place'. The second part of the pun is as important as the first. Utopias of enduring interest like More's do not function as blueprints. They combine the expression of an ideal with social criticism and freewheeling speculation. They are both tract and fiction, and as fiction they are fabulous rather than realistic.

A Modern Utopia, Wells's most substantial venture in this field, is partly a tract and does contain some fairly penetrating criticism (such as the chapter on 'Race in Utopia,' all the more welcome after some of the racist assumptions which infect *Anticipations* and *When the Sleeper Wakes*). Wells made a point of discouraging idealistic young readers who took his ideas too literally (see *First and Last Things* Bk III, Ch. 11). For all this, he does try to depict his ideal order as a lived experience. The result, though often interesting, tends to emphasise the utopia's two-dimensionality and leads to awkward formal problems. An opening 'Note to the Reader' confesses that Wells has been forced to aim for a sort of 'lucid vagueness'. A section entitled 'The Owner of the Voice' dissociates him from the narrator and his sometimes strident tone. Wells's lecture to the Oxford Philosophical Society is appended to the book as an attempt to indicate the ultimate conceptual difficulties entailed.

The presentation is correspondingly disjointed. The narrator begins by lecturing in a hall on the subject of utopias. In doing this he hypothetically takes on the role of a powerless outsider suddenly transported to another planet that is identical to our own but for its utopian culture, which he struggles to comprehend. He is accompanied by a conventionally minded botanist who rejects his idealism. The botanist finally dispels the utopia and the two men find themselves in Trafalgar Square. Their exploration is now explained as a conversation begun on holiday in Switzerland, elaborated with reference to the world about them and transformed into an alternative world in the imagination of the narrator.

The shifting framework does allow a strong measure of uncertainty and openness to offset the book's totalitarian bias, but the final effect is evasive rather than genuinely complex. In order to hold out a credible goal, Wells has to convince us and himself that we are being shown a self-consistent ideal society which he cannot quite bring into focus. What we actually see is a myth incapable of resolving the issues to which it is applied. The highlighting of sceptical, liberal attitudes does not fundamentally alter the nature of the Platonic, one-party state behind them, with its ruling elite, the Samurai, explicitly modelled on Plato's Guardians. For the Samurai, only one version of reality is valid: theirs. Truth is not to be established by critical discussions to which any citizen is a potential contributor. It is a faith into which suitably receptive individuals may be initiated. The utopia was brought violently into being by a Samurai rebellion against existing governments and retains the structure that was imposed then. There is no provision for opposition to the status quo based on conflicts of interest or opinion. Dissenters are considered to be selfish shirkers of the greater good. The two dissidents Wells portrays – the botanist, and a pianist who calls for a return to 'Nature' – are figures of fun introduced to discredit anti-utopianism in general.

When the botanist's passion destroys utopia and returns the explorers to the here-and-now, Wells is acknowledging that at present utopia is an impossibility. On the other hand, there is no suggestion that anything but the stupidity of individuals prevents it, while the squalor and suffering of our world are so intolerable that to relinquish the utopian prospect altogether seems equally impossible. Fleeing from the disheartening presence of the botanist, the narrator allows himself to imagine an angel from Revelation materialising above the Haymarket, trumpet in hand, ready to call all the potential Samurai in the world to self-realisation and action; but the comical extravagance of the image only leads him to see the limits of utopianism more clearly. This is not the age of miracles. Each ideal world that individuals envisage now is bound to be something of a personal fantasy, though a workable synthesis of them may, he speculates, emerge in time.

A Modern Utopia is by far the best of Wells's utopian books because its author, conscious of the pitfalls before him, is always ready to execute a smart sidestep into irony. The book is less a set of proposals than an intelligent discussion of utopian ideas and of Wells's ambivalent attachment to them. Some years later Wells succumbed to the temptation to produce further utopian books, with the element of irony damagingly reduced.

The orderly world of *Men Like Gods* may be confined to a fourth dimension and impossible to duplicate in this world, but there is a worrying vagueness about how far it might be approximated. Since it took five centuries of violence to establish and keeps a detailed record of all its citizens' movements, it would certainly be worth knowing which of its features are for export. At best its novelties – tame beasts and nudity – seem irrelevant because Wells has again produced a millenium rather than a utopia, only for his realism to discredit the myth. In order to distract attention from this, he again introduces anti-utopian figures of fun onto whom scepticism may be deflected. A party of narrow-minded earthlings tries to conquer the ideal world under the leadership of one Rupert Catskill, loosely based on Winston Churchill. The ensuing conflict makes the book moderately entertaining but cannot redeem it as a serious work of imagination or political thought.

When Wells revives his dissolving views comparison in *The Shape of Things to Come* it is no longer to acknowledge the uncertainty of what is coming. The future historian, whose work is supposedly revealed to one of Wells's friends in a series of dreams, is able to write confidently from the far side of the transitional period, pitying the 'divided mind' of twentieth century thinkers (Bk I, Ch. 2). Sadly what this superior observer has to tell us is modelled very crudely on events from the past. The Air Dictatorship which imposes order after the collapse of present-day civilisation is also known as the 'Puritan Tyranny'. It resolutely pursues one version of reality. All games are abolished. All books which might suggest unorthodox patterns of behaviour are suppressed. A habitually unironic expression is conferred on the human face. Even Wells finds this absolutism distasteful, declaring he would probably have been among

the actively protesting spirits who squirmed in the pitilessly benevolent grip of the Air Dictatorship. (Bk IV, Ch. 4)

He makes some attempt at critical detachment through the notebooks of Theotocopulous, a twenty-first-century Leonardo. After the possibility of significant backsliding is past, a revisionist coup even undoes some of the Dictatorship's worst excesses. But these are marginal concessions to doubt. The book fails to come to terms either with the political questions it raises or with Wells's own ambivalence.

The only one of Wells's later fantasies to entirely avoid such failure is a comparatively early one, from 1908, *The War in the Air*. The narrator is supposedly looking back from an orderly world state but all the action takes place in a much nearer future of social disintegration. The book follows the adventures of Bert Smallways, a semi-honest bicycle dealer turned beach entertainer, who is accidentally carried from Britain to Germany is a hot-air balloon. Briefly mistaken for the inventor of a coveted new flying machine, Bert is then taken to the United States by an invading German airship fleet. The Chinese and Japanese intervene in the conflict and a world war develops, followed by the collapse of industrial civilisation. After taking his revenge on militarism by shooting the German leader at Niagara Falls, Bert makes his way back to Britain and is reunited with his sweetheart, Edna.

Bert's bewildered journeying round the world combines the unique and the typical. He lives out a subjective reponse to key events, while the narrator adds clarification and polemic to underline the very real dangers of the Edwardian arms race. More naturally than in *When the Sleeper Wakes*, the movement between overview and involvement can be synchronised to the physical ascents and descents of the protagonist.

Although Wells proposes that a world state might contain the forces of disintegration which Bert's adventures reveal, *The War in the Air* does not try to jump ahead to millenial solutions. Reliance on apocalyptic ideas is mocked outright when a disabled German airship, with its crew singing a hymn to sustain morale, passes above a camp of 'born again' Canadian lumberjacks.

In so many respects it was like their idea of the Second Advent, and then again in so many respects it wasn't. They stared at its passage, awestricken and perplexed beyond their power of words. The hymn ceased. Then after a long interval a voice came out of heaven. 'Vat id diss blace here galled itself; vat?' (Ch. 7:4)

The comical voice fills the space where divine revelation should be. The airship is out of control and the words of the hymn which its crew are singing, *Ein feste Burg ist unser Gott* ('A safe stronghold our God is still'), seem highly ironic.

Since *The War in the Air* relies more on statement, less on symbol, than the earlier science fiction, there is no need to examine it at length. Sufficient to make the point that it resembles the earlier work in drawing on Christian imagery without attempting to secularise Christian beliefs. Contrary to the opinion of many commentators, for whom *The War in the Air* is an awkward anomaly, Wells's later fiction is not impoverished by the desire to convey a lesson, but by the injudicious use of Platonic and Christian mythology with which this project is usually associated. *The War in the Air* is highly didactic but succeeds both as propaganda and as fiction. No one who has read the book will be likely to forget Bert's knockabout adventures with bicycles in the early part or the eerily detailed accounts of aerial warfare later. The book is no less remarkable for intelligence than for comedy and imagination. As Samuel Hynes has pointed out, Wells was the only writer to suggest that the next big war might be global in scale and to foresee the kind of aerial bombardment which would occur in the Second World War.[20]

In one respect the later *World Set Free* (1914) displays an even more remarkable foresight, since it predicts atomic power and the atomic bomb. However, Wells passes all too rapidly from this informed speculation to pseudo-religious prophecy of the worst kind. Following an atomic war, national sovereignty is abandoned in favour of an authoritarian world state. The antichrist King of the Balkans objects, but after his extermination an ideal world emerges. The book's final chapter centres on a prophet of scientific progress who, almost like Doctor Moreau, looks ahead to the ultimate redemption of the human race by surgery.

Such bold utopianism is unlikely to appeal when viewed from the other end of the twentieth century. Science has indeed progressed in the ways foretold by Wells, producing aircraft, tanks, heat rays, spacecraft and atomic power. World wars have been followed by revolutions in which elites manipulate the masses and, sometimes at least, as in *The Shape of Things to Come*, ease their fanaticism with the passage of the years. All of this has been accompanied by suffering on a vast scale, with precious little sign of an earthly paradise to come; Wells's reputation as an advanced thinker has sunk accordingly.

There remain two big points to be made in Wells's favour, nonetheless. In writing of radical change, catastrophe and totalitarianism, he managed to foresee some of the most authentic themes and images of our era. The solutions with which he responded to the prospect ahead may carry little conviction, but in this they are no worse than the solutions of others. At his best, moreover, he also opposed to the nightmare of history resilient characters like Bert Smallways, whose sense of fun, yearning for personal fulfilment and mistrust of generalisation are an implicit rebuke to all those elite-controlled utopias which aim to absorb the individual into a collective. The period of *In the Days of the Comet* and *A Modern Utopia* is also, significantly, the period of *Kipps* and *Mr Polly*.

6

'Joy de Vive':
The Comic Novels

Many of the book reviews which the master of the scientific romance wrote during the 1890s dismiss the romance as an inferior type of fiction (*Literary Criticism* pp. 50–1 and 226–7). Admittedly it was the romance as practised by other writers which Wells disliked – Rider Haggard especially. He may have tacitly exempted his own brand from charges of escapism. Even so, he did regard the realistic novel as a worthier, more respectable and more substantial kind of fiction. The novel allowed a comparatively direct engagement with social reality and he was keen to take advantage of that possibility. 'I want to write novels and before God I *will* write novels,' he declares in a letter of June 1900 to Arnold Bennett.[21]

An article of 1897 elaborates on his idea of what a modern novel should be. It should be plotted about some social tendency as in the work of Turgenev and should show

> a group of typical individuals at the point of action of some
> great social force, the social force in question and not the
> "hero" or "heroine" being the real operative interest of the
> story. (*Literary Criticism* p. 145)

Knowing Wells's genius for self-contradiction, we should not be too surprised to find that his novels are shaped by the quest plot of romance and are concerned with protagonists who are not only favoured above the other characters by their author, but favoured more the less representative they are. Arnold Bennett found Wells's novels so lacking in the evenly balanced sympathy their author advocated that one of his letters takes him to task for serious prejudice in *Kipps* against the ruling

class.[22] If Wells sent Bennett a replay the answer has not
survived. For an understanding of why Wells's practice could
not conform to his theory we must look in the text.

Kipps is aghast to read a novel in which a character who
behaves not unlike himself is presented as an immoral,
uncivilised cad. It is to forestall such stock responses that the
novel *Kipps* has to present the actions of its central character
sympathetically. Wells could not rely on readers sharing his
values. To present a 'new man' like Kipps impartially would be
to risk his dismissal by an unperceptive public.

As in the scientific romances, Wells challenges preconceptions
by appealing to the imagination. Where the science fiction
deals in the fantastic, the comic novels deal in the romantically
improbable. The central character gradually becomes something
of a hero, passing through a series of testing adventures toward
fulfilment. His life takes on the shape of a quest and, as it does
so, the realistic novel grows to be an ironic romance. Since any
hero's struggle against a villain can symbolise all struggles
between good and evil, the implicit pattern behind any quest
plot is the age-old struggle between deliverer and devil.[23] In
Kipps and *Mr Polly* ironic romance verges at times on ironic
myth, revealing as it does so a family likeness between the
comic novels and the science fiction.

Once more we must discriminate the figurative use of such
patterns from the more literal interest in apocalypse Wells
sometimes shows as narrator. This order-seeking utopianism
tends to be rather at odds with the eccentric vitality of the
central characters, but fortunately the conflict rarely comes to
the fore. The narrator is more concerned to point out the
shortcomings of the fictional characters than to promote views
of his own. In practice his generalisations establish that the
happiness of individuals has to be achieved within the contexts
of society and nature. Wells never clearly puts the question,
how those external realities and the individual's inner life might
best be related to each other. If he did it would become
apparent that the prospect for any mutual transformation is
poor. The ideal of his heroes is a daydream which the enclosing
social and cosmic worlds might just allow to come true, but, if
so, only through chance.

The title of Wells's first comic novel, *The Wheels of Chance*,
refers to the opening up of such an opportunity and, as the

wheels of fate turn, its subsequent loss. It also refers, more humbly, to the bicycle which enables that opportunity to be taken. Wells himself was a keen cyclist who enjoyed the chance of a ride away from his labours into the countryside. He designed a kind of tandem on which he and Jane could travel round together. In Wells's novels the bicycle always appears as a vehicle of liberation. Even the time machine seems to reproduce its shape.

The cyclist whose holiday we share in *The Wheels of Chance* is a draper's assistant called Mr Hoopdriver, who is a victim of that social specialisation which Wells was later to parody in the distortion of the Selenites. He cannot discard his shop mannerisms and phrases even while on holiday. By chance he is able to act out, however, the compensatory fantasies which have become his refuge from limitation and inhibition. He rescues an attractive but rather unworldly girl called Jessie from her would-be seducer, then takes up her suggestion that he might be a colonial and dazzles her with gratifyingly extravagant tales of life in Africa.

Much of the book's comedy comes from the evident distance between such wild pretensions and the truth. However, Wells is adamant that Hoopdriver's daydreaming is more than a laughable weakness. Like his own drapery dreaming, it is a way of surviving in a hostile environment:

> his real life was absolutely uninteresting, and if he had faced it as realistically as such people do in Mr Gissing's novels, he would probably have come by way of drink to suicide in the course of a year. But that was just what he had the natural wisdom not to do. On the contrary, he was always decorating his existence with imaginative tags, hopes and poses, deliberate and yet quite effectual self-deceptions [. . . .] (Ch. 10)

We enjoy Hoopdriver's unexpected success in enacting these inner desires, sympathise at his failure to 'write' them permanently into reality.

However, according to the narrator, social reality itself is an equivalent self-deception, a set of conventions sustained by mere faith. Beneath the appearance of civilisation lie malleable primitive energies, the Palaeolithic 'natural man' glimpsed in

both Hoopdriver and the seducer Bechamel as they compete for
Jessie. In the long term such energies might perhaps be
channelled into more just forms.

How has the short-term liberation of Hoopdriver become
possible? One factor is technological progress and the
accompanying growth of the mass market, represented by
Hoopdriver's bicycle and cycling costume. Jessie and an ostler
can mistake Hoopdriver for Bechamel, even if one does so at a
distance and the other in the dark. Bechamel definitely sees in
Hoopdriver's classless clothes a threat to his own status.
Nonetheless Hoopdriver's release from social constriction is
chiefly due to chance. At the end of the book he has to
relinquish Jessie's friendship and return to his menial work at
the drapery. The only way he might escape permanently seems
to be by becoming more educated, substituting ambition and
analysis for reverie. Whether he possesses enough will power
and talent to do this successfully is doubtful.

To anyone who has read this entertaining novel, my
abstraction of it here may seem unduly gloomy. This is because,
as in the science fiction Wells was writing in the 1890s, he takes
great care to mute the dispiriting implications of his story. By
patronising Hoopdriver (a strategy begun simply enough with
his silly name) Wells is able to extract a great deal of comedy
from a bad situation he knew at first hand: that of being an
undernourished, poorly educated, sexually frustrated shop
worker with no apparent prospect of success. In the scientific
romances everyday futility is set against a backdrop of cosmic
disruption which affords us the pleasure of seeing the world
rocked and the complacent brought down. Hoopdriver's luck
does not run so far. He is trapped inside a rigid social order.
His inner fantasies are never connected to any fourth-
dimensional reality outside himself. His imaginative quest for
individual fulfilment is not linked to any more powerful, general
challenge to the status quo.

That no such link may be attainable at all is the very
unWellsian premise behind *Love and Mr Lewisham*. The ambitions
and ideals of George Lewisham, a student at the Normal School
of Science in the early 1890s, are Wells's own, but his utopianism
is sketched in unexpectedly lightly. The novel is more concerned
with the mundane experience which Lewisham is eventually
forced to acknowledge as his true element: a world of

whortleberry jam, gas lamps, reusable collars, cheap lodgings and young love. The novel represents a step down a passage Wells did not take, one which, had he done so, might have made him into a novelist rather like his friends Gissing and Bennett, chronicling the lives of apparently unremarkable middle-class people.

The one character in the book who does stand out against normal reality is the impudent spirit-medium Chaffery. The opposition between his spiritualism and Lewisham's science seems at first to be a straightforward contrast between deception and truth. But, confronted by the indignant accusations of Lewisham, Chaffery persuasively argues that confidence trickery is no more false than any system of beliefs or rules which controls human behaviour, as these are never based on simple truth but on the convenience of those who rule.

> Lies are the mortar that bind the savage individual man into the social masonry. (Ch. 23)

The argument greatly resembles Wells's in 'Human Evolution, an Artificial Process', except that Wells's utopian goal is silently abandoned as one of the lies Chaffery sees through. Chaffery does not believe the world can be perfected and so does not work on behalf of underprivileged people such as Hoopdriver. Instead he becomes a high-spirited maker of fictions who uses his talents for entirely selfish ends. While the idealistic student Lewisham hopes that socialism will one day do away with injustice, Chaffery declares that intelligent people should recognise and embrace the inevitable. By abandoning their moral integrity they will at least keep their intellects clear.

Chaffery may free himself from a false social mythology, but having nothing better to put in its place he also surrenders himself to the primitve motivation of nature. For all his engaging eloquence, Chaffery is a selfish rogue who ruthlessly exploits other people. He forces his step-daughter Ethel to assist him in his fake seances; Lewisham, in contrast, loves her and marries her. On his final appearance in the book Chaffery suggests that there may after all be a way of life which could avoid the alternative errors of irresponsibility and conformity to an unjust world. Someone who had a sound enough will might be able to contrive a course which was satisfying for himself and yet useful to his fellows. Unfortunately he does not have such a will himself. Having delivered these heartening thoughts, he absconds with stolen money, leaving Lewisham to support Mrs Chaffery as well as Ethel.

Lewisham's contrary determination to live honourably does not exactly encourage utopian hope either. From the very beginning of the book when we see him as a young schoolmaster, struggling to live up to a schema of things to learn and do, discrepancies are apparent between the specific situations in which Lewisham finds himself and his grandiose guiding theories. If his ideas are not fundamentally wrong, they are certainly disproportionate. At the same time we are expected to sympathise with Lewisham's socialism as a more honourable and intelligent response to the world around him than casual acceptance of injustice would be.

If any cannier outlook is possible, Lewisham is in no position to develop it. The pressures he is under force him to choose between his marriage to Ethel, on the one hand, or the pursuit of science and politics, on the other. His choice of Ethel is a positive settlement with reality, but there is no getting away from the fact that it is also a submission to injustice. In an ideal world Lewisham would have been able to develop both sides of his life. At the very end of the novel Lewisham speculates that mankind may be slowly progressing toward such a world, but his speech expresses hope rather than conviction. The view that a total transformation of society is a necessary and attainable goal and the view that it is a self-indulgent fantasy are left in a slack opposition, without any intermediate possibility being raised.

This novel is unique for Wells in suggesting that love between individuals, rather than mystical political commitment, is the most authentic way of conferring meaning on existence. Love is a biological imperative, a fundamental channel of human energy, 'that elusive something that threaded it together' (Ch. 15), but love is powerless to change the world and can even help to reinforce its evils, as Lewisham finds when he has to conform to suit Ethel.

Of course Lewisham stands for a way of life Wells himself had rejected just as much as does Chaffery. Wells had left his first wife in order not to be a Lewisham. Finding Lewisham's love more attractive than Chaffery's cynicism, he tries to do justice to the better of his two alternative selves; yet the love is presented rather sentimentally and Chaffery's arguments are effectively left unanswered. The novel pretends to endorse Lewisham and condemn Chaffery, but this is a simplification which evades serious exploration of their rival views. The novel itself is not greatly damaged by the evasion since, like the early scientific romances, it submerges its message within conventional plot developments, and on this level the book retains considerable charm.

Kipps is also about a choice of life, but it does not present that choice in such intellectual terms. Lewisham's wish to develop a consistent outlook may lead us to expect some kind of statement at the conclusion of his story, but the ideal against which Kipps tacitly measures experience has no connection with such Wellsian matters as science or the future. It is the imaginative world of childhood play, when he conspired with his friend Sid to impose fantasies on mundane reality, transforming a wrecked ship into the setting for imaginary naval adventures, so escaping the repressive worlds of school, church and home.

At the age of fourteen Kipps finds himself subject to a more thoroughgoing form of repression when he is apprenticed to the Folkestone Drapery Bazaar, sacrificed to the 'Moloch of Retail Trade' (Bk I, Ch. 1:2). The owner of the shop, Shalford, runs his business to an irrational system which takes no account of his employees' human needs.

When a chance to escape presents itself, the intelligence and will to seize it come, interestingly, not from Kipps, but an actor-dramatist named Harry Chitterlow. Chitterlow is an amusingly disruptive figure whose vitality is associated with rule-breaking and intoxication. Even his house is

> held up between two larger ones, like a drunken man between policemen. (Bk I, Ch. 4:1)

He enters the story by running into Kipps on a bicycle. When Kipps generously declines to call the attention of a passing policeman to the absence of a lamp on the bike, he spontaneously quits Shalford's mean world for the expansive one of Chitterlow.

Instead of deforming life to fit some rigid system, Chitterlow gives it fresh meaning through imaginative embellishments like the future success as a playwright he envisages for himself. He manages to temporarily transform Kipps too by plying him with whisky, but intoxication is an escapist solution which carries unpleasant consequences. Kipps returns to work next morning with a hangover and is sacked.

Soon after, Chitterlow stumbles on a means of transformation with greater possibilities: a legacy of £26,000 which Kipps has been left. The obscure origin and the quest for one's true identity are traditional elements of romance, but in the frustratingly realistic world of the novel true identity is not easily achieved. Kipps's vertical mobility tends to impose another false identity on him as he strains to live up to his new station, making him a comically affected figure. The upper class conventions he seeks to follow seem all the more absurd because his snobbish mentor Chester Coote has to reduce them for Kipps's benefit to a jumble of arbitrary rules. To the reader, who has been led to identify with Kipps even as a child, the customs of the ruling class are bound to appear unnatural and insincere. The fact that Society admits Kipps because he has become wealthy shows that its concern for fine discriminations in manners is a facade concealing a much more fundamental concern for finance. This is dramatised when Helen Walsingham, who had rather patronised Kipps as a pupil in her wood-carving class, rapidly becomes his fiancee.

For Kipps the right course of action remains hard to discover. If he cannot happily subdue himself to the rituals which would gain him membership of Society, such as 'Making a Call', he cannot simply return to his old way of life either, especially after Coote has forced him to give 'the Cut' to a couple of old friends. His alienation is demonstrated when he wanders through London unable to get food because, on the one hand, he is too richly dressed to enter a fried fish shop and, on the other, he is uncertain how to order and consume a meal in a restaurant. His plight is like that of the Invisible Man, who also has to go hungry in London because he dares not disclose his monstrously transformed state.

In contrast to Griffin, Kipps finds a way to get back in touch with other people and their values through a chance meeting with his childhood friend Sid, who is now a bicycle-maker and a socialist. Together Sid's Dickensian hospitality and the revolutionary views of his lodger, Masterman, identify the conventions of Society as life-impairing. But finally it is Kipps's lower-class origin which impels him to break off his engagement and quit Coote's world. Leaving an 'anagram tea', he symbolically throws away the label that bears his name in a disarranged form, then descends to the servants' quarters and proposes marriage to his childhood sweetheart Ann, Sid's sister, who is employed there as a maid.

Since even Wells's less sympathetic commentators tend to accept the love of Kipps and Ann, it is important to point out that Wells is unable to portray their love from within. Kipps and Ann are two sets of quaint mannerisms performing comic business, not two people sharing an experience. This is most evidently so when Kipps proposes, weeping extravagantly, while Anne stays contrastingly practical. The scene asks for patronage, not empathy.

> 'I been so mis'bel,' said Kipps, giving himself vent. 'Oh! I *been* so mis'bel, Ann!'
> 'Be quiet,' said Ann, holding his poor blubbering head tightly to her heaving shoulder, herself all a-quiver; 'be quiet. She's there! Listenin'. She'll 'ear you, Artie, on the stairs . . . '
> (Bk II, Ch. 8:5)

When Kipps threatens to kill himself, it is not out of love but shallow self-pity. Our identification with Kipps and Ann against the established order is liable to make us endorse the vitality of their love without reflecting that it is presented little more persuasively than the empty social rituals to which it is opposed.

Nor is it able to challenge these on their own ground. Kipps and Ann are still part of society and must accommodate themselves to society's expectations. We see this in their failure either to find a congenial home or to have a satisfactory one built for them. Their ideals are eclipsed by the pompous preconceptions of the architect, a defeat made easier by a leftover element of pretension in Kipps himself which, repeatedly thwarted, drives him to fits of anger and eventually brings the marriage close to breakdown.

Kipps is only able to find a satisfying way of life when his legacy has been squandered by his solicitor and the unfinished house sold off. He is not to be the creator of new worlds. He finds a quiet niche for himself in the old one by taking on a bookshop, cushioned against the pressures of the market by additional income from the surprise success of Chitterlow's play in which he invested during his period of wealth. Kipps's happiness does not follow from a course of action open to everyone. It is a unique situation, contrived in order to provide a happy ending to his story.

Kipps is not compromised in the eyes of the reader because his liberation is morally justified by his openness and generosity and, like Hoopdriver's, is chiefly attributable to luck. If he had been intelligent enough to rise in some other way – for example, by getting promotion, or passing examinations as Wells did – there is a danger he would seem to be betraying the exploited class of his origin. In doing this he would have ceased to be quaint but at the expense of moral shrinkage, becoming like the draper William in Wells's story 'The Jilting of Jane'. William deserts a servant girl like Ann for a more advantageous match with a milliner, after his employer introduces him to Samuel Smiles' writings on self-help. (The servant girl, proud of his intellectual accomplishments, innocently announces, 'Smiles, 'Elp Yourself, it's called .... but it ain't comic'). In *Kipps* Coote first appears delivering a lecture on self-help to people who are too poor and overworked to take advantage of it and are therefore those most in need of state intervention.

Although Kipps is not blamed for achieving success on an individualistic basis, the general issue is not ignored. Sid points out that Kipps's legacy is part of the unjust distribution of wealth and suggests that money could be put to better use by founding an Owenite profit-sharing factory. It is characteristic of Wells's mistrust of the labour movement that he makes Sid's socialism (or perhaps social democracy) Owenite – a form he considered relatively free of class-war mongering – despite the apparent anachronism involved. (Robert Owen's *New View of Society* appeared in 1813.) Kipps has a vague sympathy for Sid's ideas, but never manages to relate them to his own experiences, any more than he assimilates the 'new view of humanity' revealed to him by an anatomical illustration (Bk II, Ch. 1:4).

The challenge socialism and science present to the existing order is not integrated with the intuitive rebellion of Kipps, but juxtaposed with it through the speeches of Sid's friend Masterman. Masterman himself admits that a revolution does not seem likely, so in the few years before scientific progress brings the social order to collapse it is presumably only lucky people like Kipps who will find happiness, despite Masterman's warnings against selfishly going it alone. Masterman is not, as his name might seem to suggest, the representative of an emerging elite, but a thwarted and embittered victim of injustice whose prophecies can amount to little more than 'magnificent self-pity' (Bk II, Ch. 9:1).

The novel stays comic because attention is concentrated on Kipps's personal success rather than the general predicament. As in *The Wheels of Chance* and *Love and Mr Lewisham*, the greater context is indicated only peripherally and cautiously. In the closing pages of these novels, Kipps's bookshop, Lewisham's teaching and Hoopdriver's desire for education direct us out of their particular lives toward a fresh exchange of ideas. The novels are meant to encourage this enquiry, not to supply general solutions.

Hoopdriver, Lewisham and Kipps all resemble the young Wells in their frustrations, but they diverge curiously from Wells in the ways of life they make for themselves. Only Chaffery the confidence trickster and Chitterlow the actor-dramatist possess an imagination and will power sufficient for them to change the world to suit themselves as Wells did, and they are confined to a few glowing appearances in their respective novels. The quirky, playful kind of liberation they represent seems very difficult for Wells to reconcile with the responsible, collective aims of his utopian politics.

David Lodge has shrewdly suggested that Wells's abrupt social advancement must have left him with substantial feelings of guilt. To achieve individual success he had cut himself off from his social origins, turned from what he considered the constructive world of science to the more frivolous world of art, and, it might be added, sacrificed his love for his first wife. When he later denied he had ever been committed to his art, and turned himself into a repetitious propagandist, he seems to have been trying to reshape the nature of his success, to acquire an identity and a place in society he could better live with.[24] The playing down of the con man Chaffery and the word juggler Chitterlow are part of this process.

Rather than accept that his own career resulted from a mixture of talent and luck, Wells set about reconstructing history and career alike until the latter could plausibly stand as a microcosm of the former. Eventually he would feel able to describe himself as 'the conscious Common Man of his time and culture' (*EA* Ch. 7:1). Kipps's liberation also implies a general trend toward greater social efficiency and justice. Fortunately the point is not laboured. Wells is more concerned at this stage to do artistic justice to the texture of his experiences and the result is a rags-to-riches romance told with great verve and invention, which remains one of the best loved of Edwardian novels.

The History of Mr Polly is a still greater success because in it Wells does for once combine a comic rebelliousness like that of Kipps with a transforming imagination like Chitterlow's. Alfred Polly is consequently Wells's most heroic, most memorable and least patronised character. Unlike most of Wells's later heroes, he retains his political innocence, attempting to improve the world in ways which are intuitive and unconnected with generalisation. His aim is not to build a utopia but to promote the life-affirming species of fun which one of his friends calls '*Joy de Vive*' (Ch. 1:3). The book's appeal lies in Polly's success in transforming the realistic world of the novel into a more gratifying world of romance, while accepting the truths of conflict, suffering and individual limitation (including the limitations of Polly himself) which the realism faithfully registers.

In his childhood Polly gazes up at the stars to focus his spirit on a beauty and delight he cannot locate in his immediate experience. Playing games and reading adventure stories are the activities which make his life worth living, not the supposedly rational ones imposed on him by the school and drapery to which he is successively dispatched. The school is a world of uncomprehended lists and formulas which obscure rather than enlighten, the drapery a world of toil and routine. Wells sites the drapery in the town of Port Burdock where the Invisible Man's rebellion was finally defeated.

Polly too reacts against life's dullness, but not with ill temper and a hunger for power. He withdraws into daydreams and reads books of travel and exotic adventure. He also develops a peculiar way of speaking, which is the opposite of the ugly abbreviation and technicality favoured by Kipps's employer, Shalford. By constantly mispronoucing words Polly hopes to conceal the results of his bad schooling as affectation, but this grows into a way of colouring the world with his native exuberance, particularly aspects of the world he finds disconcerting. Thrusting competitors for jobs become the 'Shoveacious Cult' (Ch. 3:1), church dignitaries 'portly capons' (Ch. 3:2) and an unstable chair a 'friskiacious palfrey' (Ch. 5:2).

Polly's idiosyncratic responses to life invigorate a world which all about him others' conventionality is draining of meaning. For the clergyman at Polly's wedding what should be a sacred rite is a routine to be executed as quickly as possible. Phonetic spelling captures the deformity of his speech which, in contrast to Polly's lively innovations, impoverishes the experience to which it is applied.

> 'Lego hands,' said the clergyman, 'gothering? No! On book. So! Here! Pete arf me "Wis ring Ivy wed."'
> 'Wis ring Ivy wed – ' (Ch. 6:4)

Polly's unthinking mimicry of the clergyman's diction satirises it, but also marks Polly's surrender to a world of routine uninformed by creativity. His marriage is joyless and barren.

Earlier in his life there had been times when Polly was able to live in a more romantic spirit. He and his fellow drapery apprentices Platt and Parsons ramble the countryside together, drink, sing and read Rabelais (no doubt in Urquhart's incomparable translation), creating during their limited free time a joyful, innocent world. A country girl who gives each of them an apple unobtrusively associates it with the myth of Eden.

The happiness of the 'three Ps' ends when Parsons tries to bring 'Joy de Vive' into the world of work by creating a startlingly imaginative window display. The managing director insists it be dismantled; Parsons tries to protect it, assaults him with a roll of linen fabric and is sacked. Parsons later turns to socialism as a more sophisticated form of rebellion, but Polly, with his untrained intellect, is fascinated only by opportunities for individual fulfilment. When he notices how roads are fenced in by private property he does not turn to land socialism like the Angel in *The Wonderful Visit*; he simply longs for unenclosed roads on which he can ramble in search of delight. Chance intervenes to grant his wish. A legacy he receives on the death of his father allows him to temporarily escape from work and flee into the countryside on a bicycle, searching for some reality more in accord with his desires.

He discovers a red-headed, blue-eyed girl astride the wall of a school who at first seems receptive to his make-believe that she is a beautiful maiden and he a knight who has come to rescue her. Polly begins to hope that their mock idealisation of each other could be made real. He proposes they should marry in five years, when she has fully grown up and he has earned more money. The giggling of her friends on the other side of the wall disillusions him. Thoroughly humiliated, he turns to his rather emptily vivacious cousins the Larkins for comfort, only to repeat his error. Entertaining a sentimental vision of married bliss, he finds it hard to resist proposing to Minnie Larkins, then does propose to her sister Miriam – a misapplication of his imagination which condemns him to fifteen years of drab existence as a small-shopkeeper, relieved only by reading and daydreaming.

This in fact is the stage at which we join Polly at the beginning of the book. We next see how he got into this situation, then, picking up from where we left off, how he eventually triumphs over it. When Polly's business becomes insolvent he decides to burn the shop down and kill himself, disguising the two crimes as a single accident so the unsuspecting Miriam will receive the insurance money. However, as he makes his preparations, the prospect of death gives the possibilities of life a new clarity and power. The fire, once started, shocks him into a healthy reaction against the meaningless suffering he has prescribed for himself.

Instead of signalling his defeat, the fire now expresses his defiance, as it transforms the aimless, repetitious life of Fishbourne into a comic chaos. (A fascination with the elemental, transforming power of fire runs through Wells's work, as V. S. Pritchett has noted – *Critical Essays* pp. 32–3.) From the destruction Polly emerges like some god in a fertility myth.

[. . . .] Mr Polly descended into the world again out of the conflagration he had lit to be his funeral-pyre, moist, excited, and tremendously alive, amidst a tempest of applause. (Ch. 8:4)

Not only does he manage to escape suspicion of arson, but by rescuing an old lady from next door he becomes a public hero. He also becomes a saviour in the eyes of many of his neighbours because by razing their insured property he has accidentally given them a clean start in life. The loose-fitting trousers he is given after scorching his old ones prompt him to comment, 'Like being born again. Naked came I into the world' (Ch. 8:5).

Polly's rebirth is exemplary and Wells as narrator makes sure we take its meaning.

> But when a man has once broken through the paper walls of everyday circumstance, those unsubstantial walls that hold so many of us securely prisoned from the cradle to the grave, he has made a discovery. If the world does not please you, *you can change it.* (Ch. 9:1)

The whole passage is one of Wells's most forceful statements of his belief in the revolutionary power of will, yet it has no political content. It is appropriate then that Polly moves to the edge of society by becoming a tramp. Admittedly he is more of a daydream tramp than a real one. Instead of discomfort and insecurity, he discovers a carefree life and after a while finds a congenial position for himself as an 'odd man' at the idyllic Potwell Inn. His idyll is rudely shattered, however, by the arrival of the landlady's delinquent nephew, Jim. Polly realises that he still has responsibilities and agrees to defend the peace he has found.

Polly's entertaining battles with Jim parody the climactic death struggle traditional in romance. The conflict falls into the customary three stages, with Jim as the demonic antagonist that the hero must overcome in order to complete his quest.[23] Although Polly does not actually kill Jim, he does try to kill him and Jim does drown after their last encounter, effectively fulfilling the pattern.

When Polly has to decide whether or not to face up to Jim, there is an unmistakeable move toward the mythic.

> It was as if God and Heaven waited over him, and all the earth was expectation. (Ch. 9:7)

As our champion, Polly is also Everyman. His decision typifies all such decisions, as Wells again makes clear.

> Man comes into life to seek and find his sufficient beauty, to serve it, to win and increase it, to fight for it, to face anything and dare anything for it, counting death as nothing so long as the dying eyes still turn to it.

In the concluding chapter, after Jim's decomposing corpse has been mistaken for Polly's, there is a subliminal suggestion that Polly's commitment to the ideal has enabled him to break out of the ordinary world altogether. When he returns to Fishbourne and reveals himself to Miriam he tells her, 'I'm a Visitant from Another World', and refers to himself as 'a ghost' (Ch. 10:2). It is not stretching things to associate this, however gingerly, with the resurrection of Christ, since on the same page, when Polly goes back to the inn, it is mentioned that 'three poplars rose clear and harmonious against the sky' (Ch. 10:3), an image suggestive, perhaps unconsciously, of the Crucifixion.

All conflict and suffering seem to have been left behind, an order attained which transcends mortality.

> Mr Polly's mind was filled with the persuasion that indeed all things whatsoever must needs be satisfying and complete.

Wells persuades us of the same thing, by using symbols of satisfaction, not by offering a utopian blueprint. Mr Polly himself, being 'the skeptaceous sort', does not consider his experiences to be capable of generalisation. For him there is no one standpoint from which all actions can be judged. Our sense of right and wrong is something we build up through our individual lives. We sympathise with Polly because we regard the action from a viewpoint close to his own. He is a hero not because he follows a set of rules or commandments, but because he champions joy and creativity within particular dramatic contexts.

While pushing this nominalist view of Polly to its extreme, Wells puzzlingly also takes up a contradictory, absolutist position in much of his authorial commentary. If Polly burns his shop down, then society should burn London and Chicago so that better cities can be built in their place. At the beginning of the book Polly is set up as a microcosm of society: the indigestion caused by his wife's cooking is likened to civil disorder caused by bad management. Here comedy qualifies the comparison; elsewhere Wells does try to turn Polly into a rather crude political symbol.

Wells distances himself from his comments by reporting them as the thinking of an anonymous intellectual. He insists that, however beside the point or distasteful this figure may seem, his sociological analysis is necessary to make complete sense of Polly's adventures. Yet what Wells offers through the dummy intellectual is not serious analysis but a comparison (society is like an unhealthy, dissatisfied man) which registers the existence of social disorder but gives no real indication of how it may be remedied. Wells is aware of the *impasse*. He confesses to

a sense of floating across unbridged abysses between the general and the particular. (Ch. 7:3)

We may applaud Wells's determination to link these two aspects of life, but we have to agree with him that the gap remains. Polly's breakout from the normal world leads him into a child-like, pastoral one which cannot by any stretch of the imagination be converted into a political goal. This observation holds true for all the comic novels. Hoopdriver finds his greatest happiness cycling through the countryside, Lewisham walking there with Ethel when they first meet and Kipps in his childhood play by the sea.

It is also true of Bealby, the hero of a later comic novel, who appears 'as natural [. . . .] as a squirrel or a rabbit' in the country (Ch. 3:1). By the time Wells came to write *Bealby*, which began serialisation in the same month the British Empire entered the Great War, he had become convinced that the defence of 'sufficient beauty' was going to require a global, encyclopedic frame of reference due to the precarious complexity of modern civilisation. Having no frame of reference genuinely capable of integrating individual and collective action, he is forced to employ two loosely related plots. The main one concerns Bealby, a runaway child having various episodic adventures. He is a comic discomforter of other characters, especially mean-spirited ones, but he has little in the way of conscious intentions. He is almost sub-humanly irresponsible in his youthfulness. The tramp who enlists Bealby's aid in Chapter Six has carried such egotism into adulthood. An amusing but demonic figure who shamelessly dupes and steals from his fellow men, the tramp represents secession from society at its most negative. With him Wells finally jettisons the ideal of dropping out. Nobly opposed to him is the figure of Captain Douglas, an analytic thinker fascinated by the application of science but also fascinated by women. Douglas is forced to replay Lewisham's dilemma – love or his career – but this time the reverse decision is made.

The unity of the book depends on the tacit assumption that Bealby and Douglas are complementary in their hostility to the existing order. In fact Wells never really unites the intuitive play of the child and the purposive thinking of the scientist-soldier. This makes the book a lesser work than the other comic novels discussed in this chapter, where the individual and collective frames of reference unfold from one situation to which they are both clearly relevant and on which they open, however uncertainly, some kind of stereoscopic view.

Wells escapes self-contradiction in *Bealby* only by diverting tendentiousness into the subplot of Captain Douglas's development. The book is, as its subtitle confesses, *A Holiday*. Bealby's adventures have no direct bearing on the problems thinking adults encounter. Correspondingly Wells's attempts to come to terms with these in his later fiction have little connection with his sense of what it is to be a vital human being.

7

Something to Hold On to: The Later Fiction

Tono-Bungay represents Wells's chief attempt to write a serious novel. Where Lewisham, Kipps and Polly operate in a more restricted world than does Wells as omniscient narrator, George Ponderevo, the central character of *Tono-Bungay*, tells his own story, wrestling with the same disorders that beset Wells. This gives the book a striking immediacy. As the narrator struggles to relive his experiences and come to terms with them, the reader's imagination is engaged by the resourcefulness and energy with which this potentially overwhelming material is worked into shape. As the action becomes more recent, however, an element of incoherence in the narrator's conclusions does start to obtrude. The book is honest to a fault, for Wells does not permit himself to switch between ideas and characters so evasively as previously, nor so readily pour irony over the sticking points.

The autobiographical basis of *Tono-Bungay* is unmistakable. George's mother is the housekeeper of an eighteenth-century house modelled on Uppark. As we might expect, George's account of this stagnant world and of his upbringing there are utterly convincing. Like Wells, he grows into a rebel who sees that the older order is obsolete (its name 'Bladesover' suggests the poised sickle of Father Time) but, at this stage at least, we are warned through the dissolving views comparison that George has no privileged knowledge of what will succeed it:

the new England of our children's children is still a riddle to me. (Bk I, Ch. 1:3)

Although he strains towards the future, George cannot help

being shaped by the past. His idealistic conception of the state comes from his reading in the Bladesover library – not of Plato, for which he is too young, but of Plutarch. (Plutarch's 'Life of Lycurgus' nonetheless contains an account of Sparta, the state which Plato took as the model for his ideal.) Bladesover supplies George with a stable social order against which the failure of contemporary society to pull itself together may be measured. His aristocratic ideal is paralleled by his continuing obsession with the upper class Beatrice Normandy, for whom he falls when they are still children. At a later date the two become lovers, but she finally pronounces herself too corrupt to wed him and, to his distress, marries a wealthier man for whom she has less respect. Her fate is a symbol that the old ruling class cannot be redeemed. George revisits Bladesover to discover that the estate has passed from the decaying aristocracy to a rising commercial class whom he regards as even less capable of supplying the noble kind of leadership the country requires.

He would like to see the old landed gentry replaced by a truly meritocratic elite. Unfortunately these Spartan saviours are conspicuous by their absence. As the old system falls unceremoniously to pieces around him, George can find no noble order. Instead he is sucked into the specifically modern, urban way of life represented by London – fragmented, full of incompatibles, yet also highly stimulating, an existence where one must think on one's feet, be dynamic and open to new ideas. George learns to flourish in this environment, but deeply mistrusts it. He repeatedly compares its unorganised abundance to the proliferation of a cancer and wonders whether it will ever take on a meaningful shape, a question which also applies to the social structure of the nation and to his individual life. David Lodge has shown that the recurrent disease imagery helps give the book a kind of unity, while allowing George's apparently formless recollections to convey the bewildering quality of his experience (*Critical Essays* pp. 110–39). The disease imagery, and the shifts in its application from individual to city to society, may be of doubtful value as analysis, but carries great conviction as a description of George's experience and does much to hold the wide-ranging narrative together.

'It may be I see decay all about me,' George admits, 'because I am, in a sense, decay' (Bk IV, Ch. 3:1). Since he is offering himself as a symptomatic figure, his complaints against society are intriguingly self-reflexive. Extreme social mobility liberates him from uncritical orthodoxy – lets him stand back and examine life as a 'succession of samples' (Bk I, Ch. 1:1) – but at the same time leaves him obviously alienated and unsettled. His marriage fails; his career is repeatedly subject to interruptions and unexpected turns. The novel is an anatomy of George Ponderevo and his inner disorder as much as an anatomy of the social organism.

> I suppose what I'm really trying to render is nothing more nor less than Life – as one man has found it. I want to tell – *myself*, and my impressions of the thing as a whole [. . . .] (Bk I, Ch. 1:2)

George's sudden sweeping pronouncements resemble Graham's in *When the Sleeper Wakes*, but this time constitute an openly fallible attempt to understand, not excuses to peddle an apocalyptic remedy.

Significantly the novel is named after an utterly spurious remedy for man's ills, a patent medicine created by George's uncle Edward, out of which Wells teases all manner of implications. The enormous commercial success of Tono-Bungay, for example, points to the existence of a public which is unhealthy and uninformed because the state takes insufficient responsibility for its protection. The addition of strychnine, the Invisible Man's favourite tonic, to the lozenge form of Tono-Bungay shows how unregulated competition can lead to the exploitation of customers. It suggests furthermore that Tono-Bungay is a chemical refuge from a life lacking in form and meaning, comparable to Beatrice's reliance on the sedative chloral which, taken in large enough doses, can be addictive or fatal. George realises that even he is not exempt from the general malaise when he finds he is too fearful to test-fly an experimental glider he has built. Instead of resorting to a tranquilliser, he frees himself from fear and the dominance of his uncle by walking along the wall of Edward's country house in a trial of self-discipline. (This episode would have benefited, it must be said, from a rather more dramatic treatment than Wells gives it.)

For George the pursuit of personal integrity and of scientific truth are complementary ways to probe deeper into reality.

Aeronautics, favourably contrasted with the opportunistic capitalism which finances it, is almost sacred to him. When he is courageously piloting his gliders and airships he seems to be physically and mentally freed from inherited situations and constricting frames of reference, raised to an exhilarating superiority over them, like the soaring Angel at the start of *The Wonderful Visit*, Graham surveying his domain from an aircraft in *When the Sleeper Wakes* or the narrator of 'Under the Knife' floating free of the whole universe.

If such exciting liberation has a tendency to turn rapidly into alienation, depriving Wells's heroes of their human context and exposing their inconsistencies, it does at the same time expose the devitalising nature of that little world below. George is equivocal about the ultimate worth of his quest for personal integrity and of his scientific research, which leads to his injury in a balloon crash; both can still be contrasted with the entirely spurious values associated with Tono-Bungay. These are representative, and symbolic, of the unsoundness of the present social order. Since its laws and customs are not anchored in some kind of absolute, it seems to George that they must be no more substantial than the chemical formula for Tono-Bungay or than the financial structure of Edward's business.

George's view of society as a conspiracy of falsehoods recalls Chaffery's in *Love and Mr Lewisham*, but his uncle resembles Chaffery still more closely, for Edward Ponderevo is both an irresponsible manipulator of others' beliefs and a figure of unusual vitality asserting himself against an impoverishing world. We can regard him sympathetically because, unlike Chaffery, he is naive enough to deceive himself as well as others, resorting to Tono-Bungay when his health and confidence begin to fail him. Edward is a false but sincere prophet whose rebellion against the old order interestingly parallels that of his nephew.

The success and failure of his business enterprise is as much linked with the motif of ascent and descent as are George's aeronautical experiments. Edward is no sober businessman but a creative genius who finds the principal outlet for his near-boundless energy in 'the Romance of Commerce' (Bk I, Ch. 3:1). His desire to change the world is evident in his early period as a local chemist when he projects 'the Ponderevo Patent Flat, a Machine you can Live in' (Bk I, Ch. 2:4), a phrase anticipating the architect Le Corbusier by some fifteen years. George's artist friend Ewart exclaims of Tono-Bungay:

> That's what this – in the highest sense – muck stands for!
> The hunger to be – for once – really alive – to the
> fingertips! . . . . (Bk II, Ch. 3:2)

With no constructive social order or revolutionary programme to channel his energies, Edward burgeons into an irresponsible business magnate, whose goals are mere self-glorification and the cornering of markets.

Rejecting his destructive commercialism, George seeks elsewhere for the ideal, only to suffer a series of disillusionments. Love is one of the first ideals to give way, although the most persuasive expression of values in the book remains the good humour displayed by Edward's wife Susan, whose quiet loyalty stands in implicit contrast to the self-important behaviour of both the male Ponderevos. Her habitual use of the diminutive 'old' expresses the affectionate irreverence by which she distances herself from a world of overreachers. She mocks Edward's pretensions quite effectively and briskly parts him from his mistress; but the power of her love is purely domestic. It puts no restraint on her husband's career. As for George, he finds very little satisfaction in love. When his marriage breaks up he suffers suicidal thoughts over its failure.

> I had what the old theologians call a "conviction of sin." I sought salvation – not perhaps in the formulae a Methodist preacher would recognise – but salvation nevertheless. (Bk II, Ch. 4:10)

Religion itself is permanently tainted for George by his childhood encounters with a cousin's family. These bigots look forward to the Day of Judgment as a validation of their own squalid, small-minded existence, when all the fine things in life will be destroyed and their possessors damned, a belief which George rejects as a jealous fantasy.

He is more sympathetic to the creative aims of socialism, yet on inspection he discovers the most likely vehicle for socialism, the Fabian Society, is a retiring, inward-looking organisation unequal to society's immense problems – a judgment which reflects Wells's own recent attempts to convert the Fabians into a mass movement for social change.[25] George comes to doubt whether socialism will ever secure enough faith to seriously affect society. In any case, for one of his temperament it is too concerned with short-term manoeuvring and personalities; it offers no total, totally reliable scheme.

When George turns to science in his search for a firm standpoint he tells Edward,

> I want something to hold on to. I shall go amok if I don't get it. I'm a different sort of beast from you. You float in all this bunkum. *I* feel like a man floundering in a universe of soapsuds, up and down, east and west. I can't stand it. (Bk II, Ch. 4:10)

George's remark echoes the earlier cry 'I'm afloat!', with which Edward greeted the commercial success of Tono-Bungay (Bk II, Ch. 2:1). When Edward's business fails and, in so doing, seems to show the fate awaiting all order which is less than total, the floating motif appears again: George goes on a desperate sea voyage to try to put the Ponderevo enterprise on a scientifically secure foundation.

His goal is a West African island where there is a heap of 'quap', a rare radioactive mineral which can supposedly be used to make filaments of incomparable quality. When he reaches the goal of this quest George discovers, however, that quap is a terrifying epitome of disintegration.

> It is in matter exactly what the decay of our old culture is in society, a loss of traditions and distinctions and assured reactions. (Bk III, Ch. 4:5)

Under the influence of quap George shoots a native in the back and kills him – an act which he afterwards feels to have been pointless, random, unconnected with anything else in his life. This fantastic episode transposes a principal theme of the book, the inhospitality of the real to the ideal, into stark symbolic terms, but its frequent poverty of style and over-reliance on Conrad's *Heart of Darkness* for a model, seem to indicate some uncertainty or wariness on Wells's part as to the episode's significance.

Actually the most far-reaching implication is that any permanent form of order is impossible. Man's sense of right and wrong and the material world on which it is based are both shown to be subject to change. The episode entails a tacit admission that the nominalism Wells uses to discredit the existing order, by arguing that the rules may not apply to any particular case, must discredit any replacement order equally. However, although Wells's imagination pursues George's disillusionment to its logical conclusion, he does not consciously acknowledge that his own nominalist-absolutist philosophy is coming to pieces and needs to be rethought. The episode generates no fresh ideas, only a feeling of inescapable doom.

The cargo of quap rots the timbers of the ship on the return voyage and sinks it. When George at last manages to get to England he finds his uncle's corrupt business empire is also on its way down. The Ponderevos try to escape from the authorities by crossing the Channel in an airship which George has built but, in a final repetition of the sinking motif, their flight ends in a barely controlled descent, after which the airship disappears beneath the waves. Once they do reach France, Edward dies.

Money, love, religion, politics and finally science all seem to have failed George. The possibility remains that as a writer he might turn to the creative imagination and the works of art it can produce as a last, limited way of defying the flux of experience. But, despite the affinity he claims to have had since childhood with his artist friend Ewart – an affinity so great he sometimes confuses the contents of their two minds! – George finds art painfully insufficient. Art offers merely a pleasing ordering of information, not the revelation of a better world. Even Ewart himself seems to admit that he and Edward are in a similar, image-producing business.

Throughout the first and best-written part of the book George's life follows Wells's, then where Wells turned to literary interests, George enters the world of quack medicine. This suggests that at one level *Tono-Bungay* ought to stand for art and Edward for the wayward imagination which produces it. Like the confidence trickster Chaffery in *Love and Mr Lewisham*, Edward surely embodies Wells's deep fear that the artist too is a plausible charlatan, purveying a species of drug which might make people feel a little better but which, far from offering them a cure, serves only to distract them from the truths of life.

Tellingly, the death of Edward is modelled on that of the novelist George Gissing, whose classical education Wells thought a sadly out of date and irrelevant piece of equipment with which to have to confront modern reality (*EA* Ch. 8:3).

Since we are not expected to identify with Edward, he is easy enough for Wells to dispose of: a comic figure deliriously muttering fragments of egotistical fantasy and convincing himself there is an afterlife. George is more problematic, as in *Tono-Bungay* there is no distinction between narrator and protagonist. Unlike the Time Traveller or the Angel in *The Wonderful Visit* (or, for that matter, Jesus, who is presumably their ultimate model), George cannot heroically disappear into a fourth dimension, redeeming his individual failure to change the world by revealing a greater reality poised to challenge it in the future. Without such a fourth dimensional prospect where is George left? To use a horribly apt phrase, he is all at sea.

George builds an experimental destroyer and steers it down the Thames on a test voyage, which is also a fresh rejoinder to the sinking motif and the threat of dissolution it presents. He looks over the passing landscape in an embittered mood, interpreting it as a cross-section of English culture and condemning what it represents until at last, at the mouth of the Thames, he goes beyond it altogether. Despite some careless phrasing, the episode is a stirring one. It marks George's liberation from the 'windy, perplexing shoals and channels' in which he has always been forced to live (Bk I, Ch. 1:2). However, what he substitutes for the maze of frustrations is merely an image from Romantic convention: the hero spurning the petty world of his fellow men for a sublime scene where he can commune with his own soul.

George has in fact nowhere better than the ordinary world to go, and beneath the dazzling play of events and ideas which surround him he is therefore a tragic figure. He believes – like his creator, Wells – that, if the bestial nature of man is to be disciplined, culture developed with integrity and a truly just social order created, man's ideas of right and wrong must be sanctioned by some sort of quasi-transcendent authority. Yet his own prophetic quest fails to lead him to any such authority.

Because Wells cannot bear to admit this, three of the last paragraphs are given over to a grandiose, halting affirmation, unconnected with what has preceded it, expressing a vague

faith in science, art, politics, indeed all culture, as the growing
Mind of the Race.

> I do not know what it is, this something, except that it is
> supreme. It is a something, a quality, an element, one may
> find now in colours, now in forms, now in sounds, now in
> thoughts. It emerges from life with each year one lives and
> feels, and generation by generation and age by age, but the
> how and why of it are all beyond the compass of my
> mind. . . . (Bk IV, Ch. 3:3)

No doubt many people have some such progressive faith, and
minus the power fantasy of the destroyer it is not a demonstrably
foolish one. Nonetheless, placed at the climax of this particular
story, it is forced to carry a weight which its vagueness cannot
possibly sustain. George's life history brings a wide range of
subjects into a provisional, illuminating relationship which is
fascinating to read. His final attempt to extract a rousing
conclusion works only as a gesture of despair and an act of
defiance against the established order. Wells's success in *Tono-
Bungay* as elsewhere depends on contriving a balance between
earnest generalisation and playful particularity, here partly
separated out in the mentalities of George and Edward. As
Patrick Parrinder has succinctly put it,

> *Tono-Bungay* remains a rich and exhilarating novel as long as
> it has two contrasted heroes; at the end, when Edward has
> left for his heavenly mansion, it is overwhelmed by a single,
> garrulous performance. (Parrinder p. 78)

Wells's artistic decline after 1910 is essentially a continuation
of this would-be singlemindedness, a George-style outpouring
of observation and uplift, through which the lively, subversive
voice of a Polly or an Edward can sometimes, all too rarely, be
heard.

One factor in the narrowing of Wells's inspiration was
presumably the growing urgency of the world situation. Yet
Wells's artistic decline is evident some time before the Great
War and, far from concentrating on non-fictional polemic, he
continued to produce novels at an astonishing rate. It is
probably more accurate to say that by about 1910 Wells had

used up as source material all the formative experiences he really cared about. Without these particulars to be true to, and with his unwieldy history packed into a single frame of reference in *Tono-Bungay* (however insecurely), the way was open for him to restate his achieved world view with less rendering of experience and more discussion of it.

This had not been Wells's intention. In a lecture given to the *Times* Book Club in 1911, 'The Scope of the Novel' (revised and retitled 'The Contemporary Novel' for collection in *An Englishman Looks at the World*) he maintains that the novel is an important instrument of reform because it exhibits individuals in their social contexts. Since this is so, it is important that the author should not indulge in obstructive preaching, although he may profitably 'discuss, point out, plead, and display' (*Literary Criticism* p. 204). At first sight this might indeed seem to be the formula which Wells's later novels follow. The life and thought of a central character serves as the basis for consideration of the world they inhabit and of various attitudes that can be taken toward it. *Ann Veronica* is an example of the approach at its best. Although an early chapter is entitled 'Ann Veronica Gathers Points of View', a later one 'In Perspective', the book does present events in their own right, rather than in the cursory fashion of the later Wells. True, there is a contrived happy ending, and Wells identifies insufficiently with his protagonist to work up real imaginative intensity; nonetheless, it remains an accomplished minor novel, still readable, and still read as an index of women's changing place in society.

More commonly, as Wells himself had to admit, his preoccupation with the general frame of reference was such that 'the splintering frame began to get into the picture' (*EA* Ch. 7:5). In order to concentration on his alternative world view, he found it necessary to 'abandon questions of individuation' and introduce 'impossibly explicit monologues and duologues'. These do, needless to say, contain occasional felicities of phrase and observation, but they never rise to the level of wit and elegance displayed by really successful discursive writers such as Peacock, Shaw or Aldous Huxley.

When one of Wells's later novels, *The Dream*, depicts a thwarted contemporary life from within, it fatally takes as its basic point of reference the inauthentic ideal world of *Men Like Gods* in which the protagonist is merely dreaming of twentieth-

century futility and sorrow. Even so locally skilful a work as
Joan and Peter is not structured so as to unfold the experiences of
its characters but to provide opportunity for Wellsian comment
and discussion. Commentary and story impede each other's
development, so that the book's real function becomes, as
Henry James warned Wells, merely to register its author's
current state of mind.[26]

Any confusion in that mind is disguised, either by dividing
what is effectively an incoherent monologue between different
characters, or by allocating it to a single verbose protagonist
and applying an uncertain degree of irony. We might call the
latter approach the 'George Ponderevo Method'. It is used in
two memorable novels with more than a passing resemblance
to *Tono-Bungay*: *The New Machiavelli* and *Mr Britling Sees It
Through*. Both books have a central character transparently
modelled on their author, who struggles to come to terms with
experiences similar to ones which Wells found too painful to
contain easily within his system of ideas. *The New Machiavelli*
draws on his failed attempt to reconstruct the Fabian Society
and his love affair with Amber Reeves, *Mr Britling* on his
ambivalent response to the Great War.

The narrator-protagonist of *The New Machiavelli*, Richard
Remington, is a statesman setting out a retrospective view of
his career, with little awareness that there are other standpoints
than his own from which he might be persuasively criticised.
His failure to achieve political power because his sexual passion
overcomes his sense of duty and responsibility does suggest that
his opinions are going to require some ironic interpretation, but
Wells fails to indicate at what point we should become
suspicious. Much as George Ponderevo tries to clarify his
standpoint by dissenting from that of his uncle Edward, so
Remington dissents from that of his former political colleagues
Oscar and Altiora Bailey (a caricature of the Fabians, Sidney
and Beatrice Webb), criticising them outspokenly for applying
a single, reductive frame of reference to reality. Yet his own
views are inconsistent rather than more sophisticated, and there
is little evidence save the adulation of his fictitious contemporaries
to suggest either his political thought or his capability as an
administrator is inspired. He is treacherous to his wife and
colleagues; when a Member of Parliament he shows little
concern for his constituents; at one point he prays for a war to

foster world reconstruction. His only tangible contribution to political debate is the coinage of vacuous slogans such as 'Love and fine thinking'.

The third-person narrative of *Mr Britling Sees It Through* encourages more detachment from its protagonist and this book is correspondingly more successful. Hugh Britling, a well-known author, presides over a lively household in the Essex village of Matching's Easy (matching, in fact, Little Easton where Wells was currently domiciled), a household which the reader initially explores through the eyes of an American visitor, Mr Direck. At the outbreak of war Britling writes an optimistic pamphlet entitled *And Now War Ends*, corresponding to Wells's *The War That Will End War*. Britling perceives that the conflict can only conclude in a just and secure world order if mass opinion is mobilised to press for the appropriate war aims, but the swift collapse of German imperialism he anticipates, and hopes will be followed by a world conference 'and – the Millenium' (Bk II, Ch. 1:16) does not materialise, while the British ruling class proves neither so idealistic nor so efficient as he at first assumed. Britling becomes increasingly disillusioned, especially after his son has enlisted and sent back letters making plain the squalor, misconduct and dehumanisation that life in the army entails. Nonetheless, Britling's goal of world reconstruction remains disturbingly constant. Worse still, it is presented in a highly confused fashion.

Britling reluctantly welcomes the war on the ground that it challenges the indiscipline and frivolity of his own circle and, beyond them, the nation as a whole. Yet his way of life is attractive precisely because it is informal, tolerant and conducive to colourful eccentricity. Much of the book's appeal comes from a loving recreation of such curious activities as the anarchic ball games Britling organises, as with equal gusto did Wells, outbursts of human exuberance all the more to be cherished because the shadow of war looms over them.

The book survives this very basic confusion of values because Britling himself is made so real. In large measure he is a self-projection by Wells, but enormous literary experience lies behind his presentation. Although Wells had not lost a son in the war, he describes the response of Britling to news of Hugh's death with moving insight. Britling's shock is not conveyed by public grief, but by his indecision as to how large a tip he should give the girl who brought the telegram. He is horribly embarrassed both by the girl's unsympathising comprehension when he gives her a large sum, then by the need to communicate the news to his son's step-mother. Such incidental tribulations stress through contrast the momentousness of Hugh's death, and establish Britling's self-conscious isolation in this emotional crisis.

Unfortunately, prophecy comes to dominate the book as Britling diverts himself from grief by continuing to write about world reconstruction, finally proclaiming his belief in a finite god, the Captain of the World Republic, in which dead individuals such as Hugh and the family's German tutor Herr Heinrich may in some sense be said to live on.

Britling's faith is qualified by juxtaposition with the response of Letty, his secretary, to news of her husband's death. Until she learns the news is false she plots to assassinate all those who have been responsible for starting the war. Her desire for vengeance is no more than a compensatory fantasy, as we are led to see through the reflections of her sister. Its only practical result can be to reduce Letty herself to pathetic eccentricity. Wells presumably intends Letty to be a foil to Britling, bringing out the superiority of his response, but in fact the resemblance is more striking than the contrast, suggesting that he too has become a crank. Wells tells us plainly that Britling's article, 'The Better Government of the World', is a preposterously ambitious piece of work motivated by the need to defend his mind against horror (Bk III, Ch. 2:1). Even Britling is aware that all he writes is weakly conceived and expressed. Dramatically the evidence of Britling's folly is negligible, however, beside Wells's own desire to find an affirmation which will snatch some hope from the war. As a result Britling and his situation are obscured, not made clearer, by the constant generalisation in which author and character engage.

In the years that followed the Great War, Wells himself consistently assumed the Britling-like persona of an 'originative intellectual worker' (*EA* Ch. 1:1) pioneering and publicising a global, progressive outlook; but he was careful to distinguish this ideal self he had created, almost like one of his fictional characters, from the larger, more complex Wells on which it was based.

It is the plan to which I work, by which I prefer to work, and by which ultimately I want to judge my performance. But quite a lot of other things have happened to me, quite a lot of other stuff goes with me and it is not for the reader to accept this purely personal criterion.

In a 1924 preface Wells splits his personality into two warring aspects, an old unregenerate self and a newly-created persona intended to supersede it.

Temperamentally he is egotistic and romantic, intellectually he is clearly aware that the egotistic and romantic must go. (Vol. 5, Atlantic Edition)

His two liveliest works of fiction in the 1920s, *Christina Alberta's Father* and *Mr Blettsworthy on Rampole Island*, are actually throwbacks in which the new impersonal commitment is paired with, and upstaged by, romantic egotistic fantasies which belong very much to the old Wells.

The central character of *Christina Alberta's Father*, Albert Preemby, is a retired laundry-owner who comes to believe he is a kind of messiah. The belief is comic, but in a sense saner than acceptance of the petty identity the world has imposed on him. From childhood Preemby resists his fate through a 'general habit of living a little askew from actual things' (Bk I, Ch. 3:1), evident in his Polly-like failure to retain correct pronunciations and in his interest in the supernatural. Preemby views the mundane as a false appearance concealing a superior reality, which must be revealed and realised.

'Things can't be what they seem,' said Mr Preemby, waving his hand with a gesture of contemptuous dismissal towards Rusthall Village, public house, lamp-posts, a policeman, a dog, a grocer's delivery-van and three passing automobiles. 'That at any rate is obvious. It would be too absurd. Infinite space; stars and so forth. Just for running about in – between meals [. . . .] Symbolical it *must* be, Christina Alberta. But of what?' (Bk I, Ch. 4:3)

Seeking contact with the ideal, Preemby takes part in a seance. A practical joker, pretending to speak in a trance, convinces him he is a reincarnation of Sargon, King of Kings, and launches him on a plan to restore the ancient Golden Age

> on the lines of the Labour programme. Only simpler and more thorough. (Bk II, Ch. 1:7)

His proposals for an instant end to war, to the exploitation of women and to the unjust distribution of wealth are meant to seem quaint, but the irony applies to the naive pursuit of the ideal rather than the ideal itself. After all, Wells was a Labour candidate at the time.

Sargon has doubts about his prophetic persona but dares not acknowledge them. To admit he is only Preemby would be to admit there is no unseen order guiding and sanctioning his idealism and self-respect. His continued allegiance to the myth is the reverse of escapist; it is a way of maintaining contact with the ideal, and he is willing to undergo a kind of martyrdom for it when the forces of authority arrive to arrest him. His 'disciples', a mob of passers-by who fail to grasp his purpose, flee. His only genuine ally, a young writer called Bobby, denies knowing him – as Peter denied knowing Jesus. Book II, Chapter 3 is entitled 'The Journey of Sargon Underneath the World', indicating that his imprisonment in an insane asylum parallels Christ's descent into hell after the crucifixion.

Eventually Sargon is rescued by Bobby and 'resurrected' to a type of new life. The progressive psychologist Devizes persuades Preemby, who is now physically dying, that his idea of Sargon was symbolic of a real truth, that the human race is collectively a king of kings who will save and rule over the world. At the same time Christina Alberta discovers her true father is not after all Preemby but Devizes, whom Wells thus makes the eponymous hero of the book.

Having completed his reorientation Preemby dies. But when he departs so does the book's centre of interest. There is no concrete examination of contemporary social reality to be substituted for his imaginative challenge, only the untried opinions of a group of radicals which are cast into doubt by their very association with Preemby's irrationality. The book attempts to advance from the imaginative and symbolic to the rational and literal, but they remain in opposition. The kind of meaning which Preemby embodies is not carried over into the world view of Devizes.

The dedication of *Mr Blettsworthy on Rampole Island* to the 'Immortal Memory of CANDIDE' and its 115-word subtitle in the eighteenth-century manner identify it as a satirical fable in the tradition of *Candide* and *Gulliver's Travels*. Blettsworthy is brought up by his rector uncle in an assured liberal culture, but when his uncle dies he falls into a contrasting world of deception and injustice. Graves, his partner in the bookselling trade, ruins the business and seduces his fiancee. Worse still, when Blettsworthy responds by attacking Graves and almost raping the girl, he discovers his own potential for violent, egotistic and immoral behaviour and he suffers a nervous breakdown.

Hoping to benefit from a change of scene, he takes a voyage on an old tramp steamer. The rough crew are unfriendly, however, and even when the ship brings him to new lands he is unable to achieve satisfying human contact. The ship becomes disabled, there is a mutiny aboard and the officers and men escape in separate vessels. The captain, who has a grudge against Blettsworthy, locks him in a cabin and leaves him to die.

Expelled from the world of humanity and forced to come to terms in some way with the raw cosmic process, Blettsworthy suffers hallucinations in which he converses with a cynical shark. He goes mad. When he is rescued from the wreck by the cannibals of Rampole Island (as he then believes them to be) and is offered a choice of blood or milk, he drinks the blood, an act which persuades them he is fit to be admitted to their fantastically unjust society. Any of its members who breaks one of innumerable taboos is subjected to the 'reproof', a blow on the head from a two-hundredweight club set with sharks' teeth. The corpse is not identified with the deceased; it is euphemistically referred to as the 'Gift of the Friend'. Such 'gifts' form the islanders' chief source of food, although they profess to abhor cannibalism and regard it as the greatest vice of their enemies.

As the tribe's Sacred Madman, Blettsworthy tries vainly to become the prophet of a more generous way of life, but he cannot bring anyone else to believe there is an alternative to the island's wilful squalor. His special status as a tolerated eccentric is used by Chit the soothsayer as a way to overcome obstructive customs, but the new practices Chit wishes to introduce are all to do with greater efficiency in warfare. This perversion of Blettsworthy's good intentions reflects Wells's view that during the Great War the cosmopolitan aims of committed writers like himself had been encouraged for publicity purposes by politicians whose real goals were nationalistic.

Blettsworthy's means of escape is a highly unexpected one. The island turns out to have been a delusion based on his experience of Manhattan. All minds select and interpret experience, but Blettsworthy's has been so severely shocked by rampant injustice that it has created a protective fiction, transferring and confining an unbearable reality to a remote fantasy world. He is forcibly reminded that horror is at home anywhere when he becomes a soldier in the Great War and loses a leg in battle. Against this dismaying reality, the love of an American girl which allowed him to extricate himself from the Rampole Island delusion seems hardly sufficient to prevent him once more returning to it. All that protects him from a relapse is his tentative projection of an ideal world in the future. Curiously the spokesman for this desperate faith is none other than Graves, the man who originally betrayed him. The confidence with which Graves expounds his new doctrine of progress is indistinguishable from the glibness he formerly showed as a confidence trickster – an enormous, but apparently unconscious, irony.

The movement from an idealism which expresses itself in fantasising toward a more rational programme for reconstruction is common in Wells's later works of fiction, but generally his mistrust of the imagination cripples these books severely and there is little point is discussing them in a general study.

Something should be said, however, concerning Wells's discussion novels which, like the utopias, fall between the categories of fiction and non-fiction. In effect *A Modern Utopia* doubles as the first of them. The other three are loosely based on classics also: *Boon* on *The New Republic* by W. H. Mallock, *The Undying Fire* on the Book of Job and *The Anatomy of Frustration* on Burton's *Anatomy of Melancholy*. All these models – the *Republic* included – belong to a broad category of prose work which Northrop Frye has termed the 'anatomy'.[27] An anatomy deals with a great variety of subject matter, showing a strong preference for ideas over action. It takes an exuberant, even obsessive delight in curious learning, enormous lists, extravagant arguments, bizarre juxtapositions of the small and the great, the lofty and the earthy, and is often playfully satirical. Frye's catalogue of anatomists contains no less than nine writers Wells admired, the more recent of them combining the anatomy with the novel's realistic rendering of life. They are Plato, Lucian, Rabelais, Swift, Sterne, Voltaire, Peacock, Flaubert and Joyce.

Wells's 'Note to the Reader' at the beginning of *A Modern Utopia* explains that his book began as a

> discussion novel, after the fashion of Peacock's (and Mr Mallock's) development of the ancient dialogue [. . . .]

An appropriately playful element is evident in this book, as it is in the *Outline of History*, the *Experiment in Autobiography* and even *The Shape of Things to Come* (with its citations of imaginary books such as *The Natural History of the Police Frame-Up*). Unfortunately, although the anatomy might seem the perfect vehicle for the later Wells, he lacks the contemplative detachment which this form demands. None of his discursive fictions manages to get its content into a sufficiently illuminating and entertaining perspective to satisfy. So much is indicated by his recourse to the work of earlier writers for structure.

Even *Boon*, the best of the three (and the one with least resemblance to its model), is incoherently divided between play and earnestness. The book is supposed to be a miscellany of stories, jottings and drawings by or about the late George Boon, compiled by his literary executor Reginald Bliss. Boon is a successful popular writer, privately disaffected from the narrow subject matter and orthodox opinions which are his stock in trade. With the coming of the Great War, Boon's wish to prophesy for a progressive race-mind becomes fiercer, but eventually the war shatters his optimism. He dies believing that the human race has failed to seize its chance of collective salvation, much as Wells himself was to die at the end of the Second World War. Commitment and scepticism are trenchantly expressed in the book, but never allowed to shed any light on each other. Bliss can detect connections between Boon's prophecy and irony; he cannot, however, decide what they are.

Boon has little narrative strength to offset this failure to come to terms with its central theme. It is therefore a slight work in its own right, although a very interesting one for students of Wells. It is generally remembered in literary circles only for its resourceful mockery of Henry James, whom Wells accuses of pursuing formal complexity at the expense of content. *Boon* demonstrates the reverse error, by tackling serious issues without a sufficiently thorough presentation of them.

Neither in the book nor in his correspondence with the aggrieved James did Wells state forcibly that his own work needed to be valued against different criteria than those applicable to the Jamesian novel. Impatient with the limits of art, he short-circuited the argument by characterising his own work as mere journalism with accidental artistic qualities.[28] Hostile critics have been happy to seize on this flagrantly untrue remark and apply it retrospectively. Wells never quite convinced himself, however, that he was not really an artist or that art was an unhealthy frivolity. He kept a folder labelled 'Whether I am a Novelist' and mulled over it, if to little conclusion, in his autobiography (*EA* Ch. 7:5).

When preparing the Atlantic Edition of his writings, a job which involved rereading his books, revising each text and supplying a preface for each volume, Wells wrote a brief short story for inclusion which I suspect may bear on the question. 'The Pearl of Love' tells of an Indian prince who wishes to construct a worthy monument to his dead queen. The Pearl of Love is the great building he finally creates after a lifetime of devoted labour. Unexpectedly, the building can only be brought to formal perfection by discarding the casket which holds the queen's remains, a step the prince, now obsessed with the building, readily takes. We realise as he does so that the building is indeed the pearl, not the oyster which encloses it; correspondingly, the queen's remains are just the incidental piece of grit about which beauty happens to have formed. If the parable expresses Wells's customary mistrust of art as a distraction from what really matters, it equally recognises that art is long, life short. When the artist's original motives have been forgotten, the finished work may come to be valued in its own right. In the context for which it was written, the story seems a grudging genuflexion to the muse, which acknowledges

that, when the demanding political questions and the urgent
private motives have receded into history, such creations as the
Time Traveller and Mr Polly may validly accrue new significance
for new readers.

8

Outlines:
The Non-Fictional Writings

Generally speaking, the more discursive Wells's fiction is, the
less it coheres, so it is something of a surprise that the non-
fictional works themselves are comparatively undamaged by
inner conflict. The reason is simple enough. They do not claim
to give a definitive presentation of their subjects, only to call
attention to important issues and suggest possible approaches
to them. Determined not to become a complacent, respectable
member of the establishment, Wells urges readers not to blindly
follow his teachings but to reach conclusions of their own. In
The Common Sense of War and Peace he declares:

> You have a backbone and a brain; your brain is as important
> as mine and probably better at most jobs; my only claim on
> your consideration is that I have specialised in trying to get
> my Outlines true. (Ch. 1)

The *Outline of History* is a case in point. It offers a provisional
patterning of events intended to challenge dangerous nationalist
or class ideologies, and is designed to be open to criticism in
turn. The original text includes footnotes in which Wells's
advisers dissent on particular matters and Wells tries to justify
his preferred view. Throughout, Wells assumes that the work of
professional historians will sooner or later refine our
understanding sufficiently to render his own statement of man's
history obsolete. In fact the *Outline* has worn remarkably well.
Its more scholarly successors have striven for greater objectivity,
but since there is no really objective way of selecting and
organising material for such a colossal enterprise the only
sensible option is the one Wells took, to create an inspirational

story – in the positive sense, a myth – recounting where we have come from and suggesting where we ought to be headed. Wells was a master of this type of exposition. E. M. Forster described the result, despite some reservations, as 'a great book' (*Critical Heritage* p. 248). Accordingly, Wells's compact version of the *Outline*, *A Short History of the World*, remains in print as a standard popular account. The later parts of his educational trilogy, *The Science of Life* and *The Work, Wealth and Happiness of Mankind*, aim for greater objectivity and have therefore been superseded by the work of more up-to-date writers, though they remain impressive testimonials to Wells's proficiency as an author and his commitment to the needs of the general reader.

Readers with special interests may still be drawn to particular non-fictional books by Wells: for example, *Little Wars* is occasionally reprinted for devotees of war-gaming with models and *The Rights of Man* may have an interest for human rights activists, while some students of Soviet history might consider it worth investigating *Russia in the Shadows* and the booklet *Stalin-Wells Talk*. Given Wells's talent and literary experience, his non-fiction, like his post-1910 fiction, is bound to contain material which retains an appeal for individual readers or which takes on contemporary relevance for a while. Admirers of the fiction who do wish to sample Wells's discursive work might profitably begin with the articles collected in *An Englishman Looks at the World* or the later *Travels of a Republican Radical in Search of Hot Water*.

No students of Wells's fiction can afford to ignore the *Experiment in Autobiography* which contains a perceptive, entertaining description of his formative years and a vigorous account of his ideas. A sequel, concerning his affairs with women, was deferred for posthumous publication, appearing in 1984 under the somewhat misleading title, *H. G. Wells in Love*. *First and Last Things* is an important attempt to formulate his beliefs, and the mental texture of Wells's old age is agreeably caught in *The Happy Turning*, a short book made up of reflections, reminiscences and whimsical fantasies. More often cited is his last book of all, *Mind at the End of Its Tether*, for its proclamation of the imminent end of human life. Reactionaries and conservatives have sometimes, perversely, interpreted this statement as an admission by the most celebrated of idealists that commitment to revolutionary social change is futile. In fact

Wells had always approached the question of man's destiny by analogy to his own life and it was quite psychologically consistent that at the end of that life he should find it impossible to see a future for mankind. Wells had in any case never believed social progress to be inevitable or even probable, only urgently desirable and necessary as a moral goal. His true last word on the subject therefore remains the one he had set down fifty years before, regarding the Time Traveller's vision of the world's end:

If that is so, it remains for us to live as though it were not so.

Wells's pioneering work in global, interdisciplinary and future-oriented thought has been taken too much for granted. Nonetheless it is unlikely that the bulk of his discursive work will again be consulted except as historical documentation. Wells was far-sighted and an expert educator, but as a thinker he relied too much on simple oppositions such as future versus past, responsibility versus subjectivity and science versus either art or politics. It is as a writer of fiction that he most creatively explores his preoccupations.

9

Conclusions:
Wells and the Imagination

If at the time of Wells's death you had looked for a critique of his fiction, the best one available would have been *The World of H. G. Wells* by Van Wyck Brooks. It had appeared thirty-one years previously. No study of comparable seriousness was to appear for another fifteen years. The reputation Wells had established for himself as a hasty and obsessive writer, restating impractical ideas with little concern for literary elegance, had long inhibited appreciation of his earlier, more substantial writings. Informed readers had come to regard Wells as a peripheral, if not discredited figure, while of course remaining familiar with his best fiction which they had read in their youth.

Appreciative comments on that fiction did exist – for example, in Geoffrey West's perceptive *Sketch for a Portrait* – but were usually occasional and undeveloped. It was more common for critics to belittle or dismiss Wells. To Virginia Woolf in two essays of the 1920s, 'Modern Fiction' and 'Mr Bennett and Mrs Brown', Wells seemed the practitioner of a crassly external realism, who failed to give his characters' inner lives the kind of sensitive rendering the modern age, or at least Virginia Woolf, demanded.[29] Even George Orwell, who recognised Wells to be one of his formative influences, still saw him in 'Wells, Hitler and the World State' (1941) as someone who undervalued the importance of the irrational and traditional in people's lives, a deficiency which made his work overconfident and superficial.[30] When in 1948, in the widely read essay 'Technique as Discovery', the academic critic Mark Schorer wrote off Wells, Defoe and Lawrence as formally inadequate and therefore deprived of necessary self-knowledge, it might have seemed that

Wells had been classified as an inferior writer against practically objective criteria.[31]

However, a 1946 obituary tribute by Jorge Luis Borges, 'The First Wells', had already opened the way for revaluation by politely dismissing Wells the social thinker and singling out for praise Wells the creator of engrossing, disturbing fantasies (*Critical Heritage*, pp. 330–2). An article of 1957, 'H. G. Wells', by Wells's son Anthony West insists that this early Wells wrote with an unflinching scepticism. The later commitment to utopianism was a comforting delusion he imposed on himself at the cost of crippling his intelligence and artistic integrity (*Critical Essays* pp. 8–24).

With the pessimistic Wells detached from the better-known optimistic one, it was possible for Bernard Bergonzi in his seminal *Early H. G. Wells* (1961) to bring him back into the fold of literary respectability by stressing the symbolistic qualities of the scientific romances. Wells's work has steadily risen in esteem since, as an increasing number of book-length studies testifies, but with attention spreading out from the early science fiction to the Edwardian fiction and even the later books, the simple division of Wells's career into a pessimistic and an optimistic phase has lost some of its value. One of the most fruitful attempts to supply an overview is Patrick Parrinder's *H. G. Wells* (1970), which examines Wells's most significant books as expressions of alternating 'hope and despair [. . . .] release and submission' (p. 22). The present volume follows in this tradition, tracing the pattern of tensions in Wells's view of the world and their effects on his art, and concludes now by examining specifically the tensions within Wells's attitudes to the imagination.

An underlying polarisation existed long before his adult elaborations of it. As early as his first surviving work, *The Desert Daisy*, written around the age of thirteen, writing is used to pleasurably bring together two apparently conflicting ways of ordering experience: imaginative manipulation of symbols and reasoned argument. The *Desert Daisy* attributes itself to two authors, Wells and 'Buss' (one of Wells's nicknames). Buss takes responsibility for the subversive comedy of the story – fantastically ridiculing kings, generals and bishops – Wells for a preface stating that Buss has now retired to Colney Hatch lunatic asylum where he is forbidden to write.

There are two significant features here which persist in Wells's adult fiction. First is the contrast between an imaginative character and a rational one. To take only the very obvious examples, this antithesis recurs in the Angel and the Vicar, Moreau and Prendick, Cavor and Bedford, and Edward and George Ponderevo. Wells's sympathies swing from one member of the pair to the other, depending on whether the imagination is construed as subversive or constructive.

Secondly, Wells interposes a fictional narrator between himself and the story. This framing of the story recurs in *The Time Machine* and *A Modern Utopia* among other places and is especially prevalent in the short stories. Immediate first-person narrative easily turns into a variation of the same technique. By projecting the story at a remove Wells not only creates a kind of sub-world where the fantastic and the realistic can more easily meet but, making one of the characters the apparent author of the story, he is able to preserve some mental space between himself and the workings of his imagination.

One particularly revealing example of framing in this respect is the short story 'The Door in the Wall'. Its narrator claims to be reporting the recollections of a cabinet minister named Lionel Wallace. In his infancy Wallace passed through a door and found beyond it a fantastic, beautiful garden where he was totally free to play. Among many marvels he was shown a book containing his whole life, not in pictures but 'realities'. By turning the pages forward Wallace unwittingly restored himself to the ordinary world, where his confusions and sufferings were only increased by his insistence that he knew of a better one. In later life the door mysteriously reappeared to him on several occasions, but each time his concern to behave responsibly or to secure worldly advantage led him to pass it by. He now declares his fierce desire to go through the door again.

Wallace's vision is linked to the creative imagination by its association with games and books. The discovery of the vision in early childhood roots it in a mentality free of reflection or abstraction, and therefore of the firm labelling of events as real or imaginary. Positive valuation of this child's-eye view of things recalls such Romantic works as Wordsworth's 'Immortality' ode.

The narrator is fascinated by Wallace's Romantic vision but

highly suspicious of it too. He confesses puzzlement at Wallace's sincerity and power to convince.

> I found myself trying to account for the flavour of reality that perplexed me in his impossible reminiscences, by supposing they did in some way suggest, present, convey – I hardly know which word to use – experiences it was otherwise impossible to tell.

Wallace takes his reminiscences literally. One night he passes through a door in a wall, believing it to be the door of his vision, only to plunge to his death down a railway excavation shaft.

Because he takes the mythic literally, Wallace literally loses his hold on reality. Yet we are not invited to feel superior to him. The narrator is rather awed by his commitment, and the story's concluding remarks allow the possibility that Wallace's vision did contain some sort of revelation. The story seems to register the importance to Wells of the imagination as a source of meaning and a motive to action, and also the impossibility of justifying the imagination as more than a distraction from serious public concerns.

Wariness toward the imagination as a potential fifth columnist of the mind is not, of course, a trait peculiar to Wells. Plato and Paine express it. There is really no need to cite philosophers, however, since it is one of the commonplaces of everyday life that the imagination should be looked on with suspicion. Most of us find it all too easy to pass across the invisible line from mental creation into daydreaming or mere neurotic fantasy. The extraordinary mythopoeic power of Wells's own imagination led him from early on into daydreaming as much as into reading and writing, and his determination to prevent his mind wandering in this way was reinforced by the frustrating circumstances of his formative years. Surrender to daydreaming or to the imaginary worlds of art might help to keep alive his dissatisfaction with the actual world of his drapery apprenticeship; but it would also use up the precious free time he needed to seek a more permanent liberation. Having had to set his mind rigidly against the imagination at this crucial stage in his life, Wells was always inclined to regress under certain kinds of pressure to a quasi-puritanical contempt for art as escapist.

The relationship between imagining other worlds and changing this one was made to look still more like a direct opposition than it might otherwise have done because his models for change were apocalyptic. If a totally authoritative standpoint is really possible, as Christianity and Plato assume, then all other standpoints must be either complementary to it or delusions, against which the faithful should be on their guard.

While *The Desert Daisy* shows Wells to be intuitively wary of the artist's role, one of his first published stories, 'The Devotee of Art', with its portrayal of an inhumanly obsessed artist, takes a positively hostile stand towards art as a futile distraction.[32] The revised (and much improved) version of this story, 'The Temptation of Harringay', takes a better humoured view of the artist, but still regards art with suspicion. Harringay is offered a Faustian pact by the portrait on which he is currently working. After a slapstick battle he manages to obliterate the tempter from the canvas, saving his soul but, in so doing, losing his chance of creating a masterpiece.

Harringay's peril is not necessarily frivolous. Following Wells's literary career from *The Desert Daisy* through to *The Happy Turning* we encounter again and again the figure of a visionary who becomes enveloped and trapped within his own vision. Buss is locked away in an asylum as a coda to the story he himself has invented; the Time Traveller is swallowed by the immense historical dimension his efforts have opened up; Griffin eludes human sight and with it human sympathy, making himself into a doomed monster; Cavor, the inventor of spaceflight, reaches the moon only to be imprisoned deep within it forever; Blettsworthy is marooned on an island in his mind; Wallace, imagining he is stepping into a paradisal garden, falls to his death down an excavation shaft. All these examples are from works already discussed, but many others could be added. In an inferior fantasy called *The Sea Lady*, for instance, Charteris, another ambitious politician in the Wallace-Remington mould, falls in love with a mermaid who eventually drags him beneath the sea. The tension between the creative and the constructive, the dread that to explore the first would undermine the second, haunts Wells's work.

In the early fiction he did find a way to glory in his imaginative power, uninhibited by any sense of self-betrayal. He justified fantasy by science. Since science suggested to him that the complex, half-understood processes of nature were capable of delivering stranger outcomes than any mere writer could hope to dream up, he felt free to replace the old-fashioned apparatus of wizardry by a fourth dimension made up equally of science and imagination, in whose capacity to work miracles it was quite possible to believe.

In sober mood, however, Wells saw through science not an infinitely fertile and manipulable universe, but a closed, mechanical one extremely difficult, if not impossible, to turn decisively to man's advantage. Breaking out of the prison of the mundane, Wells's characters can really only find themselves in a bigger, more imposing prison, even if some of them, unable to face such a truth, insist on calling it utopia and inviting us to follow them there.

It must be admitted that there is a great deal of truth behind the darker side of Wells's thinking. The tendency of serious thought in the years since he wrote has indeed been to reduce the individual to a function of material or social processes, while technology and culture have altered for good and ill at an unprecedented and bewildering rate. Readers who find Wells's Martians far-fetched should think again. They stride across the countryside like electricity pylons, tear apart communities like planners and developers, and exterminate the innocent as efficiently as any well-equipped modern army. At times when we look beyond the little enclave of our everyday transactions it is the continuing humanity of normal human beings that seems impossible.

Yet Wells is not simply an extremely perceptive prophet of doom, for his characters are never reduced all the way down to instances of general truths. Even the most incidental figures in Wells's stories are liable to sudden outbursts of eccentricity, curiosity, temper or joy. Such underdogs as Kipps, Smallways and Polly rouse a belief in Wells, and therefore in us also, that the daydreams of a small tradesman can be somehow more real than the harsh world in which others expect him to live. Blundering, incorrigible and on occasion inspired, they are infused with Wells's own vitality.

If such 'nominalist' characters offset the 'absolutist' tendencies inherent in Wells's subject matter, the same may be said of his whole approach to storytelling. The brisk pace and imaginative fecundity of Wells's best stories never let us forget that, however chilling their implications, each is still a tremendous lark. The stories are rooted in Wells's own experience, open to trivial and irrelevant events, ready to acknowledge their own fictionality and held together not such much by conscious artistry as the voice, personality and intuitions of their author (*Literary Criticism* pp. 197–8). The negative side of this approach is that when he falls into flagrant self-contradiction Wells lacks the mental discipline to untangle himself. There are times when self-expression is not a sufficient guide.

It has become almost traditional for literary critics to discuss this limitation by comparing Wells's approach to that of Henry James, since when they fell out the two set forth their credos on art in a dramatic exchange of letters. However, this approach is less productive than it may at first appear. The combatants' criticisms of each other are palpable hits; their positive assertions are more questionable. Moreover, to see the dispute as a kind of archetypal confrontation between the definitively serious artist (James) and the superficial journalist (Wells) is to pay an unintended tribute to the forcefulness of Wells's imagination. In broaching the quarrel Wells was dramatising his change of role from novelist-cum-prophet to prophet-cum-novelist. Academics, anxious to pin down literature as a rigorous, clearly bounded subject, have usually been happy to endorse the simplistic position Wells then adopted; but this is to overlook a decade-and-a-half of sincere if qualified mutual admiration between the two authors and the inconvenient fact that the supposedly philistine Wells is responsible for a more substantial contribution to literature than most of his detractors. Before James and Wells fell out they were both artists, but artists of an entirely different sort.

I wish instead to make a comparison between the outlook of Wells and that of William Blake, an earlier apocalyptic writer with whom he felt an affinity and with whom he shares a significant overlap of aim (*EA* Ch. 5:4).[33] Although Wells and Blake had a strong grasp of contemporary culture, and were quick to absorb modern technology and scientific thought into their vision, both were as keen to change the world as to depict it. Their verbal attacks on orthodoxy were wide-ranging, irreverent and informed by a heretical Christian outlook. In different ways each held an extreme version of the Romantic doctrine that salvation is not achieveable by conformity to inherited rules, but created by the efforts of the inspired. God is not thought of as an abstraction or external force but as a man, because God is by definition the ultimate development of man. Allegiance to this apocalyptic perspective gives their work a surface of philosophical detachment which never for a moment conceals their personal commitment or inhibits their engaging Cockney forthrightness. Powerful personalities shine from their work – so much so in Wells's case that he continues to appear as a character in novels, films and even television commercials.

Blake would have found much he could endorse in Wells's writings. While he called himself a Christian, Blake had no time for God the Father as many Christians conceive of Him. To Blake this god is a mythical tyrant which people project into the heavens to explain and sanction the system of irrational authority and self-limitation in which they have become enmeshed. He accordingly appears in Blake's counter-mythology as the repressive father figure Urizen or (in moments of especial irreverence) Old Nobodaddy. Wells's adolescent rejection of Our Father who breaks men on his wheel, his later parody of that figure as Doctor Moreau and his sharp distinction between 'God the Creator' and 'God the Redeemer' in the preface to *God the Invisible King* would all have delighted Blake.

However, Blake would have been dismayed to find Wells's redeemer getting embroiled in the Great War. This misreading of a secular power conflict as the coming of the apocalypse is an indication that Wells has not broken completely free of the familiar cycle by which local pressures corrupt the true spirit of rebellion into another Urizen, proclaiming (to borrow the words of Wells's *Anticipations*) 'an idea that will make killing worth the while' (Ch. 9). The depersonalisation of Wells's Invisible King into the abstract Mind of the Race, while it may make Wells's theology look a shade more plausible to twentieth-century intellects, would only have enraged Blake. It suggests that salvation entails the individual's submersion into a collective; that there are no great men, only a supposed universal man in whom we are to be humble contributory cells. For Blake, on the contrary, all creative activity, even self-sacrifice, is the work of free individuals. 'All deities reside in the human breast,' 'God only Acts & Is, in existing beings or Men' and 'those who envy or calumniate great men hate God; for there is no other God.' 'Attempting to be more than Man We become less.' (Blake pp. 153, 155, 158 and 376).

Blake's revolution begins within. His salvation is not a far-off political goal but a matter of looking at the world with inspired eyes. When enough people do this the apocalypse will have begun. The aim of the artist is therefore not to convey information as Wells assumes but to reveal an inner vision. It is not an achievement that can be brought about by simply formulating a message at the level of rational consciousness, then thrusting it carelessly into whatever medium happens to be to hand. Blake insists that the synthesising spiritual and intellectual power of great art can only be achieved through painstaking fidelity to the concrete world of the imagination. 'Poetry admits not a Letter that is Insignificant' (Blake p. 611). The true prophet must be a totally committed artist. From Blake's point of view Wells's fitful concern for style and structure is more than ominous. That Wells's books begin with enchanting conviction but tend to end comparatively feebly is only to be expected. Wells's beginnings do vivid justice to his own experiences; his endings are distorted in the direction of some general, abstract conclusion.

Blake would see Wells as doomed to fall short of his full potential as a prophetic artist because, with whatever qualification, he is prepared to entertain an absolutist world view in which the general and the externally verifiable are taken seriously at the expense of the individual and the spiritual. Given this perspective, art no longer seems to be a necessity to human fulfilment, but something marginal and frivolous, even foolish and unmanly. Wells's declaration to James that he would rather be called a journalist than an artist is a poorly disguised apostasy from his fundamental calling, naturally followed by very little good journalism but a great deal of bad art.

The charges that Wells's idealism is compromised by a totalitarian goal and his artistry by failure to value the inner world of art in its own right are to some extent supported by the present study, although I trust it has also shown that Wells produced a great deal of work which magnificently succeeds in eluding these limitations. However, if we look at Blake through

Wells's eyes, we can see that there are substantial points to be made in the other direction.

Blake's faith that being true to the inner reality is ultimately the same thing as transforming the outer one depends on a militant belief in the supernatural as a common reality underlying both. If we do not share that belief the system falls apart. From the standpoint of Wells, Blake deludes himself by not acknowledging the objectivity of the external world.

If we content ourselves with cultivating our imaginations and purging ourselves of self-restraint, paying no attention to social arrangements or scientific developments, the starving will go unfed, the oppressed continue to suffer and the whole of human life remain needlessly impoverished in countless ways. Furthermore, while a work of art weak in aesthetic coherence is unlikely to be an effective vehicle for any additional purpose, there is an equal danger in artists pursuing their unique inner vision so single-mindedly that it becomes irrelevant or unintelligible to others. Blake, by departing radically from normal terms of thought, and constructing a resolutely alternative world view, does indeed leave his most serious work incredible and inaccessible. His contemporaries ignored or derided him, while he sank into a prickly self-absorption. Only in the lofts of Bohemian poets or the dark Satanic mills of subsidised scholarship have any readers struggled with the polysyllabic mythology of his later work.

Readers of this book will probably share something of the apocalyptic idealism common to Wells and Blake. Even if we do not believe in the Day of Judgment literally, it is probably detectable as a guiding idea lurking somewhere deep in our minds. We are also likely to share Blake's strong regard for the inner life and for the importance of art. Yet we are not likely to be so confident as Blake in denying that we live in a closed, material universe, in which the inner life and art have an uncertain status. If we find ourselves thus caught between mind and matter, subject and object, art and science, we can appreciate that Wells falls short of Blake's artistic and spiritual integrity, not because he is simply slovenly and insensitive, but because he is trying to import what he can salvage of the apocalyptic vision into a world view inhospitable to it.

To read Wells as a conventional novelist is to invite disappointment and confusion because Wells craves to join the everyday details he observes to an informing cosmic scheme. The effort to do so, the failure to completely do so, and the braving of that failure, are all part of his special reality. A would-be epic writer in a mundane and fragmented liberal culture, he is only fully successful when striking an ironic balance between the domestic and the visionary. When all the reservations have been made, Wells's apocalyptic conviction that all knowledge and experience could be brought into a single liberating perspective nonetheless emboldened him to several very remarkable achievements.

In his first five years as a professional writer he transformed science fiction from a popular genre on a level with pirate or detective stories into an art form representative of its age. Such has been his influence that even writers who question his ideas have used his methods to do so: among them E. M. Forster ('The Machine Stops'), Aldous Huxley (*Brave New World*), C. S. Lewis (*Out of the Silent Planet*), George Orwell (*Nineteen Eighty-Four*) and William Golding (*Lord of the Flies* and *The Inheritors*). Outside Britain, Yevgeny Zamyatin and Jorge Luis Borges are among the most eminent authors to have shown and acknowledged Wells's influence, while in the field of popular science fiction it would be difficult to find any example of the genre from anywhere in the world, either on the page or the screen, untouched by his example.

Not only in the scientific romances but the best of the comic novels and social novels, Wells succeeded in creating fluent, highly original stories which have the facility of appealing to a wide range of readers at different levels. Such books have been, as T. S. Eliot put it, a treat for readers in the first and third class compartments alike (*Critical Heritage* p. 321). In them Wells outflanks expectations with remarkable energy and authority. *Kipps* is a fine comedy, but it is also an inside account of the disorientation suffered by the socially mobile in Edwardian England. *The War of the Worlds* is an exciting adventure story, but also displays vividly the implications of living in a secularised universe.

If Wells introduced the perspectives and implications of science into literature more forcefully than any previous writer, he also brought before cultured readers the world of the lower middle class. Hindsight inevitably notes Wells's patronage of characters like Kipps, but contemporaries such as Henry James and Vernon Lee saw clearly that Wells wrote with a new sympathy and understanding for them.

In his non-fictional books too Wells worked to overcome harmful compartmentalisations. He believed that science, politics, history, religion and economics were not closed intellectual realms, accessible only to professionals, but part of the republic of letters, relevant to everyone.

The causes his polemical works advocate are certainly not to be dismissed. There is nothing silly about respect for human rights, more efficient methods of social planning, the recognition of a global perspective or even the creation of a world state. Where Wells sometimes errs is in not arguing for these objectives on their own terms.

To transfer the synthesising vision of art into the world outside the book does not, sadly, result in a genuine blueprint for apocalypse, but incoherence: intellectual incoherence in the non-fiction, artistic in the fiction.

The defectiveness of Wells's ideal results in two towering paradoxes. Firstly, quality and earnestness become inversely proportional. The early scientific romances and the two major comic novels – works intended as entertainments – are his most accomplished, substantial achievements. His more seriously intended books are uneven and self-contradictory, faults which even the very best of them, *Tono-Bungay*, does not entirely escape. Secondly, when he appeared to desert the imagination for the more rational fields of science and politics, Wells did not become a genuine scientist or politician but an aesthete, irrationally demanding that life should possess the coherence and closure of a work of art. By not acknowledging that the idea of apocalypse is itself a fiction, and by attempting to contain the world within it, Wells condemned himself to the fate he was seeking to escape. He became a prisoner of his own terrific imagination.

His best work is that in which he uses the idea of a new, perfect world figuratively or in parody. Here he writes in the spirit he himself praised in an obituary tribute for a fellow science-journalist, J. F. Nisbet:

> to me, at least, it has a touch of the heroic, that feeling, as he certainly did, a strong attraction towards certain aspects of devotion, he would defile himself with no helpful self-

deceptions to anticipate his call, but remained, as he was meant to remain, outside, amid his riddles.[34]

Writing in this spirit, Wells produced a range of lively narratives which have delighted and inspired several generations of readers. Despite their author's own reservations, the power of these books seems likely to endure for some time yet.

Notes

1. K. R. Popper, *The Open Society and Its Enemies*, Vol. I (London: Routledge & Kegan Paul, 1966 edition) pp. 173–4. My approach to the subject of utopianism has been much influenced by this book throughout.

2. B. Russell, *Portraits from Memory* (London: Allen & Unwin, 1956) p. 80.

3. See Popper, *The Open Society and Its Enemies*, pp. 57–9.

4. T. H. Huxley, *Evolution and Ethics* (London: Macmillan, 1893). Although the lecture was given after Wells had left South Kensington, the ideas it contains were certainly familiar to him.

5. T. H. Huxley, *Method and Results* (London: Macmillan, 1893) pp. 199–250.

6. M. Arnold, *The Portable Matthew Arnold* (Harmondsworth: Penguin, 1980 edition) p. 421. Wells's remark comes from 'Scepticism of the Instrument', appended to *A Modern Utopia*.

7. Although the text of 'The Universe Rigid' was never published, Wells summarises its argument in Ch. 5:2 of the *Experiment in Autobiography* and some of it seems to have been incorporated in a version of *The Time Machine* which was serialised in the *New Review*. This and 'The Rediscovery of the Unique' are both reprinted in R. M. Philmus and D. Y. Hughes (eds.), *H. G. Wells: Early Writings in Science and Science Fiction* (Berkeley and London: University of California Press, 1975) pp. 93–4 and 22–31.

8. A giant traditionally symbolises the individual's integration into a greater, fulfilling whole; Wells makes use of the figure several times in his work. On this symbol see N. Frye, *Anatomy of Criticism* (Princeton: Princeton University Press, 1957) pp. 119 and 141–3.

9. See E. Wilson, *Axel's Castle: A Study of the Imaginative Literature of 1870–1930* (London: Collins, 1964 edition).

10. G. Hough, *The Last Romantics* (London: Duckworth, 1978 edition) pp. 263–74.

11. G. Orwell, *Collected Essays, Journalism and Letters*, Vol. I (Harmondsworth: Penguin, 1970) p. 30.

12. For the different stages of composition see D. J. Lake, 'The Drafts of *The Time Machine*, 1894', *Wellsian* 3 (1980) 6–13, and Bernard Loing, 'H. G. Wells at Work (1894–1900), Part One, *The Time Machine*', *Wellsian* 8 (1985) 30–4.

13. See P. Parrinder, '*News from Nowhere, The Time Machine* and the Break-Up of Classical Realism', *Science-Fiction Studies*, Vol. III (1976) 265–74.

14. See H. Cantril, *The Invasion from Mars* (Princeton: Princeton University...

Press, 1940); also M. Draper, 'The Martians in Ecuador', *Wellsian* 5 (1982) 35–6.

15. T. H. Huxley, *Evolution and Ethics*, pp. 22–9.

16. See *The War of the Worlds* Bk I, Ch. 7, *The New Machiavelli* Bk 3, Ch. 1:5 and *The World of William Clissold* Ch. 1:2.

17. See W. Bellamy, *The Novels of Wells, Bennett and Galsworthy, 1890–1910* (London: Routledge and Kegan Paul, 1971).

18. R. Williams, *The English Novel from Dickens to Lawrence* (London: Chatto & Windus, 1970) pp. 128–30.

19. See N. Cohn, *The Pursuit of the Millenium* (London: Maurice Temple Smith, 1970 edition) pp. 30–2, 71–4 and 111–26.

20. S. Hynes, *The Edwardian Turn of Mind* (Princeton: Princeton University Press, 1968; London: Oxford University Press, 1968) pp. 43–4.

21. H. Wilson (ed.), *Arnold Bennett and H. G. Wells* (London: Hart-Davis, 1960), p. 45.

22. Wilson, *Arnold Bennett and H. G. Wells*, p. 127.

23. On the romance, see N. Frye, *Anatomy of Criticism*, pp. 187–9.

24. D. Lodge, *The Novelist at the Crossroads* (London: Routledge & Kegan Paul, 1971) pp. 217–20.

25. Compare *Tono-Bungay* Bk II, Ch. 1:3, and 'Faults of the Fabian', reprinted in Hynes, *The Edwardian Turn of Mind*, pp. 390–409.

26. L. Edel and G. N. Ray (eds.), *Henry James and H. G. Wells* (London: Hart-Davis, 1958), p. 167.

27. N. Frye, *Anatomy of Criticism*, pp. 308–14.

28. Edel and Ray, *Henry James and H. G. Wells*, p. 264.

29. V. Woolf, *The Common Reader* (London: Hogarth Press, 1925) pp. 194–204, and *The Captain's Death Bed* (London: Hogarth Press, 1950) pp. 90–111.

30. Orwell, *Collected Essays, Journalism and Letters*, Vol. II, pp. 166–72.

31. W. V. O'Connor (ed.), *Forms of Modern Fiction* (Minneapolis and London: Minnesota University Press, 1948) pp. 9–29.

32. J. R. Hammond (ed.), *The Man with a Nose* (London: Athlone Press, 1984), pp. 50–60.

33. My reading of Blake is much indebted to N. Frye, *Fearful Symmetry: A Study of William Blake* (Princeton: Princeton University Press, 1969 edition).

34. H. G. Wells 'J.F.N.', *The Academy* (May 6th 1899) pp. 502–4.

Bibliography

SELECTED WORKS BY WELLS

Books by Wells referred to in the text are listed below. For a complete list, see
H. G. Wells: A Comprehensive Bibliography (London: H. G. Wells Society, 1986
edition).

The Time Machine (London: Heinemann, 1895).
The Wonderful Visit (London: Dent, 1895).
The Island of Doctor Moreau (London: Heinemann, 1896).
The Wheels of Chance (London: Dent, 1896).
The Invisible Man (London: Pearson, 1897). Epilogue added in first US edition
    (New York: Edward Arnold, 1897).
Certain Personal Matters (London: Lawrence & Bullen, 1897).
The War of the Worlds (London: Heinemann, 1898).
When the Sleeper Wakes (London: Harper, 1899). Revised as *The Sleeper Awakes*
    (London: Nelson, 1910).
Love and Mr Lewisham (London: Harper, 1900).
The First Men in the Moon (London: Newnes, 1901).
Anticipations (London: Chapman & Hall, 1901).
The Sea Lady (London: Methuen, 1902).
The Food of the Gods (London: Macmillan, 1904).
A Modern Utopia (London: Chapman & Hall, 1905).
Kipps (London: Macmillan, 1905).
In the Days of the Comet (London: Macmillan, 1906).
New Worlds for Old (London: Constable, 1908).
The War in the Air (London: Bell, 1908).
First and Last Things (London: Constable, 1908). Revised (London: Cassell,
    1917) and (London: Watts, 1929).
Tono-Bungay (New York: Duffield, 1908; London: Macmillan, 1909).
Ann Veronica (London: Unwin, 1909).
The History of Mr Polly (London: Nelson, 1910).
The New Machiavelli (New York: Duffield, 1910; London: John Lane, 1911).
Little Wars (London: Palmer, 1913).
An Englishman Looks at the World (London: Cassell, 1914). Published in US as
    Social Forces in England and America (New York: Harper, 1914).
The World Set Free (London: Macmillan, 1914).
The War That Will End War (London: Palmer, 1914).

Boon (London: Unwin, 1915).

Bealby (London: Methuen, 1915).

Mr Britling Sees It Through (London: Cassell, 1916).

God the Invisible King (London: Cassell, 1917).

Joan and Peter (London: Cassell, 1918).

The Undying Fire (London: Cassell, 1919).

The Outline of History (London: Newnes, 1920). Frequently revised.

Russia in the Shadows (London: Hodder & Stoughton, 1920).

A Short History of the World (London: Cassell, 1922). Revised 1946; revised 1965 by Raymond Postgate and G. P. Wells.

Men Like Gods (London: Cassell, 1923).

The Dream (London: Cape, 1924).

Christina Alberta's Father (London: Cape, 1925).

The Short Stories (London: Benn, 1927).

Mr Blettsworthy on Rampole Island (London: Benn, 1928).

The Science of Life with Julian Huxley and G. P. Wells (London: Amalgamated Press, 1930).

The Work, Wealth and Happiness of Mankind (Garden City, NY: Doubleday, 1931; London: Heinemann, 1932).

The Shape of Things to Come (London: Hutchinson, 1933).

Experiment in Autobiography (London: Gollancz & Cresset, 1934).

The Anatomy of Frustration (London: Cresset, 1936).

Travels of a Republican Radical in Search of Hot Water (Harmondsworth: Penguin, 1939).

The Rights of Man (Harmondsworth: Penguin, 1940).

The Common Sense of War and Peace (Harmondsworth: Penguin, 1940).

The Happy Turning (London: Heinemann, 1945).

Mind at the End of Its Tether (London: Heinemann, 1945).

The Desert Daisy Gordon N. Ray (ed.) (Urbana: University of Illinois, 1957).

Henry James and H. G. Wells Leon Edel and Gordon N. Ray (eds.) (Urbana: University of Illinois, 1958; London: Hart-Davis, 1958).

Arnold Bennett and H. G. Wells Harris Wilson (ed.) (Urbana: University of Illinois, 1960; London: Hart-Davis, 1960).

H. G. Wells: Early Writings in Science and Science Fiction Robert M. Philmus and David Y. Hughes (eds.) (Berkeley and London: University of California, 1975).

H. G. Wells's Literary Criticism Patrick Parrinder and Robert M. Philmus (eds.) (Brighton: Harvester, 1980; Totowa, N.J.: Barnes & Noble, 1980).

H. G. Wells in Love G. P. Wells (ed.) (London and Boston: Faber & Faber, 1984).

The Man with a Nose, and Other Uncollected Short Stories J. R. Hammond (ed.) (London: Athlone Press, 1984).

SELECTED BIOGRAPHY

Hammond, J. R. (ed.), *H. G. Wells: Interviews and Recollections* (London: Macmillan, 1980).

MacKenzie, Norman and Jeanne, *The Time Traveller* (London: Weidenfeld & Nicolson, 1973; New York: Simon & Schuster, 1973).
Smith, David, C., *H. G. Wells: Desperately Mortal* (New Haven and London: Yale University Press, 1986).
West, Geoffrey, *H. G. Wells: A Sketch for a Portrait* (London: Howe, 1930).

SELECTED CRITICISM

Batchelor, John, *H. G. Wells* (Cambridge: Cambridge University Press, 1985).
Bellamy, William, *The Novels of Wells, Bennett and Galsworthy, 1890–1910* (London: Routledge & Kegan Paul, 1971).
Bergonzi, Bernard, *The Early H. G. Wells* (Manchester: Manchester University Press, 1961; Toronto: Toronto University Press, 1961).
Bergonzi, Bernard (ed.), *H. G. Wells: A Collection of Critical Essays* (Englewood Cliffs, N.J.: Prentice-Hall, 1976).
Brooks, Van Wyck, *The World of H. G. Wells* (New York: Kennedy, 1915; London: Unwin, 1915).
Hammond, J. R., *An H. G. Wells Companion* (London: Macmillan, 1979).
Hillegas, Mark R., *The Future as Nightmare: H. G. Wells and the Anti-Utopians* (New York: Oxford University Press, 1967).
Hynes, Samuel, *The Edwardian Turn of Mind* (Princeton: Princeton University Press, 1968; London: Oxford University Press, 1968).
Kemp, Peter, *H. G. Wells and the Culminating Ape* (London: Macmillan, 1982; New York: St. Martin's Press, 1982).
Lodge, David, 'Assessing H. G. Wells' and 'Utopia and Criticism' in his *The Novelist at the Crossroads* (London: Routledge & Kegan Paul, 1971; New York: Cornell University Press, 1971).
Orwell, George, 'Wells, Hitler and the World State' and 'The Rediscovery of Europe' in his *Collected Essays, Journalism and Letters*, vol. II, Sonia Orwell and Ian Angus (eds.), (London: Secker & Warburg, 1968; New York: Harcourt, Brace, 1968).
Parrinder, Patrick, *H. G. Wells* (Edinburgh: Oliver & Boyd, 1970; New York, Putnam's, 1977).
Parrinder, Patrick (ed.), *H. G. Wells: The Critical Heritage* (London and Boston: Routledge & Kegan Paul, 1972).
Ray, Gordon N., 'H. G. Wells Tries to be a Novelist' in Ellmann, Richard (ed.), *Edwardians and Late Victorians* (New York: Columbia University Press, 1960).
Reed, John R., *The Natural History of H. G. Wells* (Athens, Ohio: Ohio University Press, 1982).
Suvin, Darko and Philmus, Robert M. (eds.), *H. G. Wells and Modern Science Fiction* (Lewisburg, Pa.: Bucknell University Press, 1977; London: Associated University Presses, 1977).
Wagar, W. Warren, *H. G. Wells and the World State* (New Haven: Yale University Press, 1961).
Williams, Raymond, *The English Novel from Dickens to Lawrence* (London: Chatto & Windus, 1970).

The *Wellsian*, a scholarly journal devoted to Wells, is published annually by the H. G. Wells Society, which may be contacted c/o the H. G. Wells Centre, Department of Language and Literature, Polytechnic of North London, Prince of Wales Road, London NW5 3LB, England.

The Wells Archive (Wells's books, letters and papers) is preserved in the Rare Book Room, University of Illinois Library, Urbana-Champaign. The most extensive collection of Wells material in Britain is held by Bromley Central Library. See A. H. Watkins (ed.), *Catalogue of the H. G. Wells Collection* (London: London Borough of Bromley Public Libraries, 1974).

Index

Learning Resources
Centre